Adventures of
COW

by
COW

as told to Lori Korchek

and photographed by Marshall Taylor

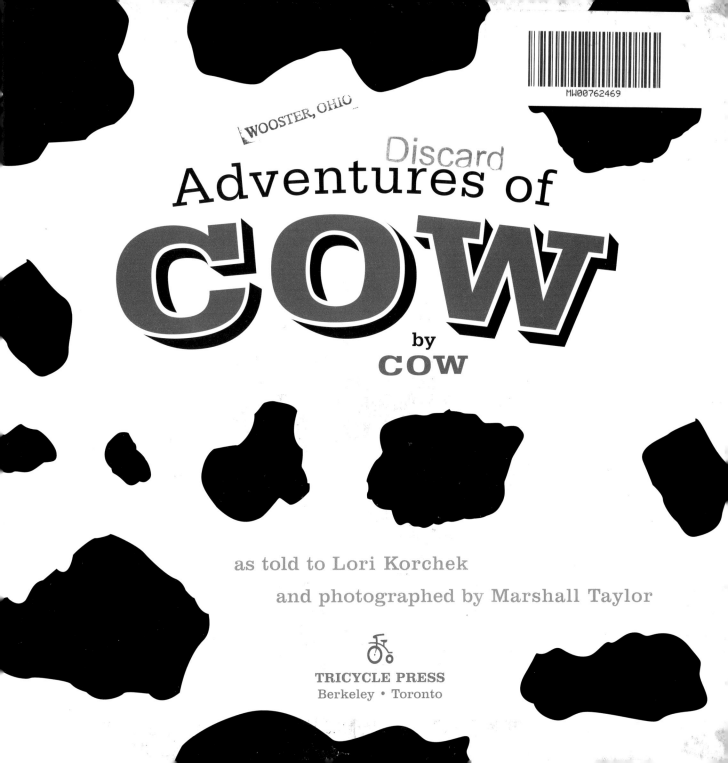

TRICYCLE PRESS
Berkeley • Toronto

After a long journey, Cow arrived in a strange land.

Cow asked some big dogs, "Where am I?"

But they didn't speak Cow.

So Cow asked a pig, "Which way is home?"

The pig said, "A-a-a-ask the cats."

"Excuse me," said Cow. "How do I get home?"

"If I were you, I'd swim," honked the cat.

So Cow tried to swim home...

but swam into a herd of scary frogs.

Thank goodness a big bird swooped down just in time and brought Cow home.

Cow's dad was waiting at the door. "Hi, Pop!"

Cow's mom was at the window. "Hi, Ma!"

"Group hug!" yelled the twins.

Aunt Ernie said, "You should write a book about your adventures."

So Cow did.

Cow became famous and was on TV.

Cow was even on magazine covers.

But Cow didn't care about all that.
Cow just wanted to play checkers.

The end.

Tricycle Press
a little division of Ten Speed Press
P.O. Box 7123
Berkeley, California 94707
www.tenspeed.com

Design by Betsy Stromberg
Typeset in Clarendon

Library of Congress Cataloging-in-Publication Data
Korchek, Lori, 1959-
  Adventures of Cow / by Cow, as told to Lori Korchek ; photographed by Marshall Taylor.
      p. cm.
  Summary: A lost cow has many grand adventures before finding her way home.
  ISBN 1-58246-139-2
  [1. Cows—Fiction. 2. Humorous stories.] I. Taylor, Marshall, 1957- ill. II. Title.
  PZ7.K83637Ad 2004
  [E]—dc22
                                        2004010275

First Tricycle Press printing, 2005
Printed in China

1 2 3 4 5 6 — 09 08 07 06 05

Adventure
SPORTS PHOTOGRAPHY

Creating Dramatic Images in Wild Places

TOM BOL

Peachpit
Press

ADVENTURE SPORTS PHOTOGRAPHY
Creating Dramatic Images in Wild Places

Tom Bol

Peachpit Press
1249 Eighth Street
Berkeley, CA 94710
510/524-2178
510/524-2221 (fax)

Find us on the Web at: www.peachpit.com
To report errors, please send a note to: errata@peachpit.com
Peachpit Press is a division of Pearson Education.

Acquisitions Editor: Ted Waitt
Project Editor: Rebecca Gulick
Development Editor: Stephen Nathans-Kelly
Copy Editor: Liz Merfeld
Production Coordinator: David Van Ness
Compositor: Kim Scott, Bumpy Design
Proofreader: Patricia Pane
Indexer: Valerie Haynes-Perry
Cover Designer: Charlene Charles-Will
Interior Designer: Charlene Charles-Will with Kim Scott, Bumpy Design

13-digit ISBN: 978-0-321-80982-7
10-digit ISBN: 0-321-80982-3

9 8 7 6 5 4 3 2 1

Printed and bound in the United States of America

This book is dedicated to my wife, Cree, and my son, Skyler.
Their endless support, patience, and encouragement have
allowed me to pursue my photography dream.

Acknowledgments

This book wouldn't have happened without a lot of help and support of others. The list is long; I'm grateful to all.

First, I'd like to thank Rebecca Gulick, Stephen Nathans-Kelly, Sara Jane Todd, Ted Waitt, Charlene Will, and all the other hard-working people at Peachpit who made this project a reality. Their tireless efforts brought my words and images to life in these pages.

I'd also like to express my gratitude to the many talented photographers who have given me sound advice during my career, including Dave Black, Peter Dennen, Patrick Endres, and the late Galen Rowell.

To the great folks I teach workshops with, including Colby Coombs, Mirjam Evers, Najat Naba, and George Theodore.

To Scott Kelby and Matt Kloskowski; their humor, energy, and knowledge are insurmountable.

To Adam Rothman, who can make even me look good on video.

To Mark Astmann, Kriss Brunngraber, and Will Holowka for their support and technical advice.

To my friends at Nikon, Lowepro, and SanDisk, who always have a solution for my precarious shooting situations.

To Steve Glass and Randy Pfizenmaier for helping me out on numerous shoots.

A lot of credit for this book goes to the outdoor athletes I've photographed through the years. They are the ones who make these images possible. I hope this book captures some of their adventurous spirit.

I'd also like to thank my family, who have always supported my interest in photography and the outdoors.

Contents

Introduction

I still vividly remember that frosty winter day I graduated from journalism school in Colorado. I had spent five years of my life learning everything there was to know about taking photographs and writing magazine articles. I was ready to conquer the world with my new education. But I had one distraction—a very big distraction. I was obsessed with adventure sports.

While my college roommates went off to job interviews in three-piece suits, I was lacing up my climbing shoes for another bouldering session. Three weeks after graduation, my roommates were settled in a nice apartment in Denver with promising careers. I was hunkered down in a tent at 20,000 feet on Aconcagua in Argentina getting ready to take National Outdoor Leadership School (NOLS) students to the summit. Ten years later, my college roommates had moved into a nice house and were very successful. I had also moved up in the world, teaching kayaking and climbing in remote parts of the world like Patagonia and the Himalayas.

I spent month after month in the backcountry pursuing my passion. My total material worth consisted of a beat-up blue Toyota truck, my climbing gear, and my cameras. No house, no cell phone, no computer. I spent my summers climbing on jagged Alaskan peaks and my winters paddling warm ocean waters along the Baja coastline. I was living the dream of a climber, kayaker, and wilderness junkie.

But then I got distracted again, this time in the opposite direction. I had always carried a camera with me to document my expeditions. But I started to notice that same creative urge I had experienced growing up and in journalism school. The desire to create got stronger and stronger. Soon my passion to create overtook my desire to climb the next peak or paddle the next river. I wanted to share my outdoor adventures with others, to communicate my deep appreciation and respect for wild places. Adventure sports and wild places had become a permanent part of my makeup. Now I needed to show the world the incredible sports taking place in some of the most beautiful places on the planet. My love of adventure sports and my passion for photography merged.

Today I'm more settled, living in a house instead of a truck. I don't spend as much time on lengthy expeditions, but I shoot more adventure sports than ever. Society has changed its views of climbers and kayakers. Instead of being viewed as outcasts, climbers and kayakers are in vogue. Indoor climbing gyms have popped up around the country and many schools have their own climbing gyms. Whitewater parks have been built in rivers, some in the middle of downtown urban areas. You can sip your Starbucks coffee, then drop right off the sidewalk into a surfing hole. The outdoor industry has become a multimillion-dollar revenue source. A photographer can make a living working in this industry.

Other things have also evolved in adventure sports photography. Digital cameras have become more advanced, allowing photographers to capture scenes that, only a few years ago, would have been unthinkable. Flash technology is rapidly advancing. High-speed-sync flash photography using studio packs has come of age. I can shoot an airborne skier at 1/2500 of a second and illuminate him 60 feet away using my Elinchrom Ranger, an impossible feat only a few years ago. Camera technology will continue to improve and open up new frontiers in adventure sports photography.

Every year I teach hundreds of students about adventure sports photography. I enjoy teaching, no doubt an offshoot of teaching wilderness skills as an outdoor instructor for so many years. Digital photography has given many new photographers the access and affordability they needed to pursue this art form. Based on questions I'm asked by students, there is a huge demand for more information and technique on shooting adventure sports. Current trends have paralleled my own progression; digital photography and adventure sports have merged for many people.

I wrote this book to answer as many of those questions as I can. I hoped to weave together some interesting personal experiences, hard-learned lessons, and a lot of useful photo technique. Learn by my mistakes. Use this book as a reference for photographing adventure sports. Take what you learn in these chapters and create stunning images, instead of mediocre snapshots. I've included many specialized techniques to elevate your image-making to the next level.

In the end, I hope this book inspires you to head outdoors and capture images of your favorite adventure sports. This may be as simple as capturing a family camping trip or documenting an expedition to an 8,000-meter peak. Maybe your college roommate never had a chance to try rock climbing. Now is your opportunity to make his hands sweat and pulse race through the images you capture on your next climb. Go out and shoot! The process is as important as the end result.

1

Pack the Right Gear

Who's going to carry all that gear?" This question is bouncing around in my head while I stare at all my equipment in the quaint bush town of McCarthy, Alaska, population 38. I'm headed into the Wrangell St. Elias National Park on assignment for *Men's Journal*. Eleven million acres of massive glaciers, unclimbed peaks, roaring rivers, and grizzly bears will be my "studio" for the next 2 weeks. I'm accompanying a group of climbers hoping to do a first ascent in a remote area of the park. Not only do I need camera gear for every angle, but also batteries, food, fuel, camping gear, radios, first-aid equipment, climbing gear, clothes, and bear spray. No base camps, road systems, pack horses, or helicopters; we'll be traveling by foot every day across this rugged landscape. Luckily for me, I was able

Hiking into Chugach State Park to capture a sunset image.

1-1 Way off the grid in Alaska.

to convince the editor I needed an extra person to help carry my camera gear. But my pack still weighs 85 pounds. Time to pack right and light.

Unlike many photography situations where there is a warm car or café nearby, adventure sports photography often takes place in very remote wilderness areas (**FIGURE 1.1**). Trips can range from day outings to months-long expeditions. In addition to your camera equipment, it's critical to pack the right clothing and camping gear to stay warm and safe in the conditions you encounter. The more comfortable you are in the field, the more you can focus on your photography and not the sound of your teeth chattering on a frigid belay ledge.

Layer It Up

When you have to carry everything on your back, your packing strategy becomes very focused. Sure, we would all like to have our favorite warm, fuzzy, cotton hoodie to wear around camp at night. But after one rainstorm that warm, fuzzy hoodie turns into a heavy mop with no insulating value. If being a wilderness fashionista is a priority, you're in luck because today many warm waterproof garments also look good. Just remember that function always trumps fashion in the backcountry (**FIGURE 1.2**). Better to be warm and dry in that boring green Gortex raincoat than become hypothermic wearing your favorite red cotton T-shirt.

1.2 Photographing the Iditarod Trail Sled Dog race in temperatures well below zero.

HOW YOUR BODY LOSES HEAT

Knowing how your body loses heat will help you layer properly for the elements. There are five ways the body loses heat: convection, conduction, radiation, evaporation, and respiration.

Convection heat loss occurs when the wind blows warm air away from your body. Adding a windproof layer to your clothing eliminates this issue.

Conduction refers to heat being drawn out of your body due to contact with a cold object, such as snow or ice. Adding a layer between you and the cold object will help.

Radiation heat loss occurs when the body loses heat to cooler items surrounding it without touching those items. Thick layers will reduce this type of heat loss.

Evaporation heat loss occurs when your sweat changes to vapor, a process that consumes body heat. Avoid overheating and sweating to minimize this form of heat loss.

Finally, *respiration* heat loss occurs when you exhale warm, moist air from your lungs into a cold environment. Your body has to warm up the cold incoming air in your lungs. Breathing through a warm face mask or balaclava will help warm the air that enters your lungs and reduce this type of heat loss.

The best approach for dressing in the field is using a layering system and sticking with fabrics that work in the backcountry. During a day of shooting in the field, conditions can vary widely, ranging from hot and sunny to cold and rainy. Using lightweight layers instead of one heavy coat allows you to effectively regulate your temperature and stay comfortable. Ideally, you don't want to sweat a lot or shiver a lot. If only that were possible! By adding or removing clothing layers you can stay more comfortable and focus on your photography.

The good news for photographers is that there are highly efficient new materials used in outdoor gear that are very warm, lightweight, and waterproof. These new garments help keep pack weight and size down. As a rule of thumb, avoid cotton unless you're shooting in a very warm environment. Down, synthetic insulation, polar fleece, and wool are good choices for the backcountry.

Down is very lightweight and efficient as an insulator, but it loses its insulation value when it gets wet. I use down a lot in the field. I'm just careful to keep it dry (**FIGURE 1.3**). If I'm working in a really wet environment, I leave my down at home. Synthetic insulation like PrimaLoft and Polarguard is also lightweight. These solutions compress well, and most importantly, insulate when wet. Synthetics don't have as much insulation value as down by weight, but they keep you warm when wet, and are more durable than down.

Fleece options are also a good choice. They're durable and warm, and they come in a variety of styles and weights. I have a trusty Patagonia Synchilla jacket I have used for years on extended expeditions, and it works as well today as it did when I bought it. Wool is another good choice. Wool has been around longer than any of the new fabrics, and on decades of expeditions it's proven very durable and warm when wet. The only downside to wool is that it's heavier than the new synthetics on the market today.

What about lightweight layers? I'll admit that if I'm on assignment, going to a warm area like the Grand Canyon, I'll bring a cotton T-shirt along in my pack. But my other lightweight hiking gear will be nylon. Nylon dries out faster, is lighter weight, and can be treated to provide sun protection. I can rinse out my nylon hiking shorts in a stream, wring out the water, and put them right back on and start hiking.

1.3 Drying out gear at a rest break on the West Buttress on Mount McKinley.

If you tried this with cotton shorts, your legs would chafe until they were bright red stalks! I also pack long-sleeve nylon shirts to avoid sun exposure. On a 3-week sea kayaking trip in Baja I'll finish tube after tube of sunscreen (**FIGURE 1.4**). But if I wear a long-sleeve shirt, I can pack a lot less sunscreen for the trip. Every ounce counts when you are carrying your own gear.

Staying dry is another important aspect of backcountry photography. Getting cold and wet is a perilous combination on remote trips. Hypothermia, a dangerous lowering of the body temperature, can occur at temperatures in the 40s, especially if you're wet. Stay dry by always packing raingear. I prefer to use raingear that breathes, which eliminates sweat buildup and keeps me dry during strenuous activities. Numerous fabrics such as Gortex allow body moisture to escape while keeping the rain out. If I'm working in really rainy conditions, I use rubber-coated raingear and "wellies" (rubber rain boots). Once, I paddled for 60 days straight in southern Chile, and day after day it rained. Helly Hansen raingear and rubber boots saved the day.

Keep your extremities warm

Special care should be taken with protecting your extremities. In the backcountry, your feet are your means of transportation; think of them as a nice set of tires. If your tires get holes in them, you're out of luck. Simple blisters can turn into evacuation-worthy infections in the backcountry. Choose boots that are comfortable and provide enough support for your travels. Break in your boots before leaving on a long trip. Use a sock system to prevent chafing and

1.4 A tough job—on assignment in Baja.

blisters. I like to use a lightweight liner sock and a heavy wool sock for most of my hiking. Bring moleskin to smooth out the hot spots on your feet when hiking. Happy feet means happy photographers, which means better images.

When working in extreme cold you need a special boot to keep your feet warm. For mountaineering you'll want a plastic boot with a warm liner. These boots are the norm for mountaineering, and allow the use of crampons for climbing. If you're standing around in the cold and aren't climbing, then use insulated pac boots by Sorel. I have stood around for hours at 20 degrees below zero photographing dog mushing in Alaska, and Sorel Glacier boots kept my feet warm. These boots are rated to 100 below; if your feet get cold in Sorel Glaciers, you must be in Antarctica (**FIGURE 1.5**).

Hands are also critical for the photographer. You need to have finger dexterity to work your camera and lenses in all conditions. The challenge arises when you're photographing in cold weather. I use a few different glove/mitten systems for cold-weather photography. If the temperature is going to be above freezing, I use a lightweight glove. These liner gloves give me great mobility and just enough protection from the cold.

1.5 A Jack London moment: photographing dog sledding in the glaciated Chugach Mountains.

If the temperature dips closer to zero, I add a heavier glove over my liner glove for more protection. I can shoot with my camera with this heavier glove on, but don't have nearly as much dexterity. For photographing in subzero weather, I wear a heavy liner glove covered by an insulating mitten. The mittens are attached to my jacket via cords so I can take them off to shoot and not have them blow away. Some mittens also have finger sections that fold back, exposing your fingers for easy camera handling. Using a liner glove with these mittens also works well in extreme cold.

Don't forget about your head. A lot of heat loss occurs through your head, so the saying goes, "When your feet are cold, put on a hat." Wear a sun hat to prevent sunburn in hot desert climates.

LAYERING TIPS

- Pack numerous layers to efficiently regulate body temperature.
- Choose down, fleece, or synthetic fabrics— all good choices for layers.
- Avoid down when you're shooting in wet environments—it loses its insulation when wet.
- Don't pack cotton layers for most backcountry situations.
- When your feet are cold, put on a hat.

What Camera Gear to Bring?

This is the million-dollar question, and the hardest one to answer! The best way to approach what camera gear to bring is to consider the shooting situation. What you carry boils down to three things: trip length, remoteness, and creative goals.

I have found that what camera gear I bring depends less on the activity and more on the remoteness of the shoot and the client. The only exception to this packing strategy is when I need to bring underwater housings for water shoots. One big question is, where are the images going—to you, or to a client? If I'm shooting on my own time for stock, I can deal with a broken lens preventing me from shooting for a day. But if I'm shooting on assignment, then I have to produce good work. Equipment failure is not an option. Backup lenses and bodies are necessary.

The creative goals of a shoot also help determine what gear to pack. If I'm photographing distant climbers, then I need a long telephoto lens. If I'm shooting mountain bikers racing right by my camera at ground level, then I need my fisheye lens. But most of my shooting—probably 80 percent—is shot between 20 and 200mm, no matter what the subject.

DETERMINING WHAT CAMERA GEAR TO BRING

- Do you have to carry all your gear, or do you have help?

- Is it a day trip, or will you be spending multiple nights in the field?

- Is it a personal shoot or a shoot for a client?

- What are the creative goals of the shoot?

Choosing cameras

Adventure sports photography is often tough on camera gear. Working in extreme environments will test the limits of your equipment's durability. Even if you take every precaution, chances are your camera will get banged, dropped, squished, soaked, wind-blasted, and frozen all in the same trip. And at the heart of your system is your camera, a piece of gear you want to choose wisely (**FIGURE 1.6**).

1.6 Choose the right camera for the job.

There are three important features to consider when you get a new camera: durability, weight, and speed. The first consideration is the durability of the camera. Cameras vary in the quality of their construction and how much weather sealing is used. Basic cameras are often built using a lot of plastic parts and are not sealed against moisture. Pro-level cameras are built primarily from metals and are well sealed against the elements. In the middle are numerous cameras offering various degrees of durability and weather sealing.

Weight (and size) is another big concern. Since many adventure sports shoots take place far away from your car, you will want a camera that is easy to carry into the field. Lighter cameras are smaller and easier to carry in your pack.

Finally, you need to consider shooting speed. Many adventure sports are fast-moving events. Imagine a kayaker paddling off a 60-foot waterfall. You're only going to get one take on this drop, so the more frames you can pack into the sequence, the better. Frame rates vary in cameras from 4 frames a second to 9 or more.

I use all Nikon 35mm cameras, including a Nikon D3 and D300s as my primary camera bodies. Both cameras are pro-level bodies, well sealed against the elements and very durable. The D3 is my choice for fast-action shooting since it shoots 9 frames a second. And in terms of durability, the D3 is hard to beat. When I need to travel lighter, I go with my D300s. I use the D300s on backcountry trips when minimizing weight is paramount. The D300s camera also shoots HD video.

I also carry another camera with me, the Nikon P7000. This is a point-and-shoot camera that cranks out amazing digital files. I can slip it into my jacket pocket for a trip to the local market and no one labels me as a photographer. If I see a great image on the street, I can use this camera to get the shot.

Lenses

The second critical part of your camera system is your lens. In choosing a lens consider four aspects: optical quality, zoom range, weight, and speed. The good news is that today, lens quality has gotten very good, even in entry-level lenses, and it's only getting better. Pro-level lenses will have a better build and more resolution, but you can still create excellent images without buying the best glass (**FIGURE 1.7**).

Another variable is the zoom range. I use many zoom lenses in my shooting. Optically, they're very good, even better than fixed focal-length lenses in

1.7 Use a variety of lenses for different perspectives.

some cases. And since they cover a range of focal lengths, they're more practical in the field. The lenses I use that aren't zooms are specialty lenses. These include the 10.5 fisheye, the 45mm PC-E tilt shift, a 1.4x TC14 II teleconverter, and an 85mm 1.4 lens.

Weight is also a concern, and this directly correlates to how fast the lens is. A fast lens has a wider aperture opening than a standard lens. For example, I often use my 70–200mm f/2.8 lens. The widest aperture opening on this lens is f/2.8, which results in a bright, fast-focusing lens. All lenses focus at their widest aperture and close down to the chosen aperture only at the moment of exposure. Since autofocus works better in bright light, an f/2.8 lens will allow better autofocus performance than an f/5.6 lens.

The downside of faster lenses is that they use larger glass elements, which makes them heavier. Fast lenses like pro f/2.8 lenses also cost more. You must decide what lenses best suit your shooting style and

fit in your budget. Rest assured that most lenses today produce sharp, vibrant images as long as your technique is good. Producing good images is about getting out in the field and shooting, shooting, and shooting. We've all heard the "if only I had this lens" excuse—I've used it a few times. Try explaining that to a client!

Flash cards and cases

Compact flash cards are the third type of gear you need to take digital photographs. When you're choosing flash cards, there are three important characteristics to consider: size, speed, and durability. Flash cards come in various capacities from 1 GB (gigabyte) to 128 GB, and they just keep getting larger. High-capacity flash cards are nice since you don't have to switch out cards very often. This is very helpful when shooting in an underwater housing. You can shoot all day and not have to purge the housing and take out your camera. The downside of using really large cards is you have all your work on one flash card. If this card gets corrupted or you lose it, then you are out of luck. How often do cards go corrupt? Very rarely, and most major flash card manufacturers have recovery software that will help you retrieve images off a corrupt card.

Speed is also important. Flash cards will label their speed rating as an "X" speed or MB/s (megabytes per second). For example, one flash card may be rated 200x while another card is rated 100 MB/s. The bottom line here is that you want as fast a card as you can afford. Certain photography situations such as shooting video or firing away at 9 frames a second require a fast card or your shooting may be

1.8 Flash cards and Gepe waterproof cases.

HOW DURABLE ARE COMPACT FLASH CARDS?

I have nightmares about compact flash cards randomly corrupting all my images. Should I be worried? The short answer is *no*. Flash cards are more durable than you might think. I've occasionally dropped my clothes into the washing machine with a flash card in my pocket. It's during the dry cycle when I hear pings in the machine that I realize my flash card just got washed. Guess what? After letting it dry out, my laundered cards have performed perfectly with no problems. Experiments have been done where flash cards have been crushed, dropped, and washed and they come through just fine. I'm not recommending dropping your flash cards in a puddle and tempting fate, but if you're concerned about losing your images, keep in mind that flash cards have shown that they can take some abuse and still work fine.

interrupted. The card won't be able to write data fast enough to keep up with your shooting.

Durability is also a factor with flash cards. Once again, choose flash cards from a reputable company, and get the most durable cards you can afford. Many flash cards get labeled "pro" or "extreme" to indicate they are more durable than basic flash cards.

I use flash cards exclusively by SanDisk (**FIGURE 1.8**). I really like SanDisk's Extreme Pro cards for their speed and durability. I use card sizes of 4 GB, 8 GB, 16 GB, and 32 GB, depending on the shoot. As cameras evolve and produce larger file sizes, I'll rely more on larger cards. It's hard to believe we could get only 36 frames on one roll of film. Now I can shoot a thousand photos on one card.

If you're in the backcountry for multiple nights, you'll need a safe place to store your flash cards. I use flash-card cases by Gepe. These cases hold four flash cards in transparent cases. The best part is these cases are completely waterproof. I've dropped a Gepe case in the ocean and watched it bob around for a few minutes until I could retrieve it. When I opened the case, the flash cards were totally dry.

The minimalist kit

I organize my camera gear into specific kits. Photographing adventure sports often involves long, strenuous hikes and technical systems. Being hindered by extra weight directly affects your ability to photograph your subjects and may jeopardize the entire shoot. For those times when weight is paramount, I go with my minimalist camera kit (**FIGURE 1.9**).

1.9 The minimalist kit.

MINIMALIST CAMERA KIT

- Nikon D300s camera body
- Nikon 24–120mm f/4 lens
- 4 16-GB SanDisk SanDisk Extreme Pro flash cards
- Lowepro Toploader Zoom 55 AW case

One camera, one lens, and 64 GB of card space. This setup covers everything from wide-angle to moderate telephoto views. Zoom lenses have gotten better through the years, allowing photographers to carry fewer lenses and still have good optical quality. Nikon's 24–120mm performs well and features *vibration reduction*. The vibration reduction (VR) feature offered in some lenses allows shooting at very slow shutter speeds and reduces the need for a tripod. This camera kit easily fits in my backpack and weighs just over 3 pounds. The disadvantage with this system is you have no backup if anything breaks. I've broken a few lenses and cameras through the years, but it doesn't happen very often.

When weight isn't a big concern, I'll add more gear to this kit. The first thing I'd add is a Nikon SB-900 speedlight and SU-800 wireless transmitter. Many times the light in the field doesn't do what you want. Using a speedlight, gives you a lot of creative lighting options. I'd also add a wide-angle zoom like the 14–24mm f/2.8, more flash cards, and a lightweight Gitzo GT1550T tripod. These additions bring your camera-gear weight to around 10 pounds, still very reasonable as a load in a backpack. I could still add a 70–200mm f/2.8 to this gear and be comfortable carrying it on a day trip.

The standard camera kit

Let's face it. Most adventure sports photography takes place close to your parked car. Maybe the location is a local climbing crag or roadside surfing hole. Having your car nearby allows you to carry the camera equipment you may need for the shoot. Here is the gear I carry in my standard camera kit (**FIGURE 1.10**).

Since weight and space aren't an issue, I bring my prime lenses, including my 200–400mm f/4 and multiple speedlights. This amount of gear will cover almost anything I shoot. The exceptions would be underwater shoots requiring housings and more lighting gear for portraits.

Remember, you don't need all this gear to make great photographs. It's much more important to actually be in the field shooting with the gear you have than at home dreaming about gear you would like. I have a colleague who can walk through a busy market in Cairo with one body and a 50mm lens and create stunning photographs. Gear is important, but the user is what makes the image.

STANDARD CAMERA KIT

- Nikon D3 and D300s camera bodies
- Nikon lenses; 10.5 fisheye, 14–24mm f/2.8, 24–70mm f/2.8, 70–200mm f/2.8, 200–400mm f/4
- 2 SB-900 speedlights
- 1 SU-800 transmitter
- 1 Gitzo GT2541 tripod with Really Right Stuff BH-55 head
- 100 GB of SanDisk Extreme Pro flash cards
- Lowepro Vertex 300 photo backpack

1.10 The standard gear I carry in my pack.

UNDERWATER CAMERA KIT

- Nikon D300s camera body
- Nikon lenses: 10.5 fisheye, 24–70mm f/2.8
- 2 SB-900 speedlights
- 3 Pocket Wizard wireless triggers
- 1 AquaTech D300s housing
- 1 AquaTech fisheye port
- 1 AquaTech 24–70mm lens port
- 2 AquaTech SB-900 housings
- 1 AquaTech Pocket Wizard Housing

The underwater kit

Shooting in the water, or underwater, requires special housings to keep gear dry. Generally, I'm close to the action when shooting in the water or underwater, so I don't need telephoto lenses. Here is what I carry on shoots involving underwater photography (**FIGURE 1.11**).

We will look more at underwater photography in Chapter 5, "Photographing Watersports."

1.11 The underwater camera kit.

Tripods and heads

Tripods are essential tools for the adventure sports photographer. Imagine shooting distant climbers on a spire with your long telephoto lens. Or light painting a desert arch with flashlights in the middle of the night. Whether you need stability using telephoto lenses or long exposures, tripods are critical in these situations.

My tripod use has declined over the years as a result of improved technology. Lens-based image stabilization (IS), or vibration reduction (VR), allows me to shoot at very slow shutter speeds and still get sharp images. High ISO camera performance also lets me shoot at ISO 3200 and use much faster

1.12 Using a tripod is critical in low-light conditions.

shutter speeds than I could use in the past. But if I'm shooting a 30-second exposure, I need a tripod to get a tack-sharp image (**FIGURE 1.12**).

I use two different tripods for my shooting, both Gitzo carbon fiber models. Carbon fiber is very lightweight and strong. It's expensive, but worth the extra dollars. When I started my career, I went through one tripod after another until I finally wound up with my two Gitzos. I've had these tripods for years and they work flawlessly. For heavy loads I use my Gitzo GT2541, and for lightweight loads I use my GT1550. The GT2541 weighs 3 pounds and folds down to about 2 feet (**FIGURE 1.13**). The 1550 packs down to 14 inches and weighs about 2 pounds, easy to carry in a backpack.

What goes on top of the tripod is also important for stability. I use ball heads by Really Right Stuff. These heads are beautifully made, solid, and reliable. They use a custom plate system for attaching camera gear to the head. I use the BH-55 for my large tripod, and the BH-30 for my small one.

1.13 For heavy loads I use a Gitzo tripod and Really Right Stuff head.

What about filters?

I like to use 3 different types of filters in the field. Some of these effects can be duplicated in the computer, but I like to do as much as I can in the field. The first filter I never leave home without is a Singh-Ray LB Color Combo Polarizer. Polarizers help saturate colors, reduce glare, and add contrast. I love how my skies pop when I use polarizers. I also use Singh-Ray graduated neutral density (ND) filters. These 4"-×-6"-rectangular filters are shaded on the top and clear on the bottom. These filters help reduce contrast you encounter at sunrise and sunset. Imagine a sunlit peak with a dark foreground. By placing the shaded part of the filter over the sun area, you reduce contrast and bring in more detail in the shadowed foreground. My favorite style is the 2-stop, soft-edged graduated ND filter.

Lastly, if I'm going to be photographing water, I bring my Singh-Ray Vari-ND filter. This filter uniformly darkens an image, allowing you to use very slow shutter speeds to enhance motion. Crashing surf and whitewater can be transformed into silky, dreamy landscapes by shooting slow shutter speeds using the Vari-ND (**FIGURE 1.14**).

1.14 The Singh-Ray Vari-ND filter allows you to use slow shutter speeds for creative effects.

How to Carry All That Gear

Once you've decided what camera gear to bring, then you have to figure out a way to carry it. Once again, there are many options, depending on how much gear you have, and how far you're carrying it. My preference for photo bags is Lowepro. Their line of bags includes everything from urban to expedition-style photo bags and backpacks. Let's start with how to pack the minimalist kit.

To pack my D300s and 24–120mm lens, I use a Lowepro Toploader Zoom 55. This simple bag holds the camera and lens snugly, and has a pocket for extra flash cards and filters. The bag also has a waterproof cover, which is critical for protecting gear in rainy conditions. The Toploader Zoom is small enough to carry in my backpack, or I can carry it around my shoulder. This bag also works well if I'm shooting while hanging on a rope. Things don't get much simpler than this.

1.15 The Lowepro Vertex 300 loaded and ready to go.

If I'm backpacking and want to carry my standard camera kit, I use the Lowepro Vertex 300. This is a large photo backpack that is comfortable to carry on long hikes, and it also fits in standard overhead compartments on planes. I can carry my 200–400mm lens in the center of the pack, and store lenses, bodies, and speedlights on the sides (**FIGURE 1.15**). This pack also has a waterproof cover.

For canoe and rafting trips I use a Lowepro Dryzone 200 backpack. These packs are completely waterproof (**FIGURE 1.16**). The nice thing about having a waterproof backpack instead of a hard case is the ability to carry your gear on hikes. I often take side hikes on rafting trips and need a backpack to carry my camera gear. The Dryzone works great for hiking.

I can carry all of these packs onto planes and not worry about rough baggage handlers. I normally bring all my camera gear as a carry-on when I travel by plane. If I need to check camera gear such as lighting equipment, I use Lowepro Pro Roller cases (**FIGURE 1.17**). These hard-sided cases have wheels and padding inside to protect gear while going through baggage check. I've carried my lighting gear numerous times in my Pro Roller and it always comes out fine on the other end.

For the roughest conditions, including wet weather and lots of bouncing around, I use Pelican cases. Pelican cases are almost indestructible, completely waterproof, and they even float. On expeditions where my equipment may be transported by mule, boat, jeep, and plane, the Pelican case is the best protection for my gear (**FIGURE 1.18**).

1.16 The Lowepro Dryzone 200 keeps gear dry while canoeing and rafting.

1.17 The Lowepro Pro Roller loaded with lighting gear ready for travel.

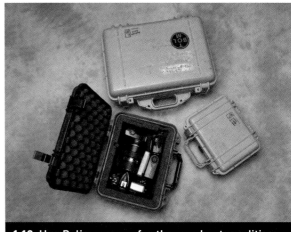

1.18 Use Pelican cases for the roughest conditions.

2 On the Road

Paul Petzold, who founded the National Outdoor Leadership School (NOLS), was a legendary mountaineer who participated in many expeditions around the world. I worked as an NOLS instructor for 14 years, taking students in the wilderness for 30 days at a time. Students would learn a variety of backcountry skills from route finding to rock climbing. One thing I learned very quickly: Planning logistics during the first couple of days was crucial to the success of the month-long expedition. As Petzold liked to say, "Prior planning prevents piss-poor performance." Boy, was he right.

Exploring the rugged Baja coastline.

Adventure sports photography projects, whether single-day excursions or month-long expeditions, always require careful planning (**FIGURE 2.1**). Nothing feels worse than getting off the plane in a distant country and realizing you forgot a lens, battery, or tripod. Diligent planning will ensure that you have the gear you need to create the images you want.

Portable Power

One issue that comes up no matter where you're going or how long you'll be traveling is powering all your camera equipment. Cameras, flashes, laptops, satellite phones, cell phones, and portable hard drives all need power. On shorter trips, it's a simple matter of bringing enough batteries. On longer, more remote photography trips, you need to be prepared to power up your gear in the field.

Start by always bringing extra camera batteries. I bring multiple camera batteries on backcountry photo trips. This allows me to shoot for up to a week before I need to recharge my batteries. I use manual focus and avoid excessive LCD image review in the field to save battery power. I always buy Nikon batteries for reliable performance. I've tried third-party batteries and had them go bad after a few months of use. I also use rechargeable batteries in my SB900 speedlights. This way I can recharge them in the field, eliminating the need to bring boxes of AA batteries.

There are excellent solar-powered panels available for recharging your electronics in the field. I use Brunton Solar Rolls for field recharging (**FIGURE 2.2**).

2.1 Getting oriented with the Alaska range in the distance.

2.2 Using a Brunton Solar Roll to recharge a camera battery.

2.3 Using a Brunton Sustain battery to recharge a cell phone.

These panels are small, waterproof, and roll up into a tube for easy transport. On a bright, sunny day, I can recharge the battery of my D300s in about 3 hours. The panels can be tethered together to speed up battery recharging.

Laptops and cell phones can also be easily recharged in the field. Brunton makes lithium batteries that can be charged from the solar roll in the field. These batteries can be used to power a laptop or cell phone. I use the Brunton Sustain battery for this job (**FIGURE 2.3**).

Traveling outside the U.S. also means the AC power supply—and plug configuration will be different. Websites such as Walkabout Travel Gear (www.walkabouttravelgear.com) have charts detailing the voltage and plug configurations of different countries. Canada and the U.S. are 110–120V countries, while many other countries use 220–240 volts. Some electronics like laptops and battery chargers

are rated for 220V (check the device for ratings). Devices rated for 220V need only the right plug style to work. If the device isn't rated for 220V, or the electricity supply is outside the normal voltage, you'll need a transformer to convert the electricity to the correct voltage. Try your local Radio Shack to purchase a plug adapter set.

Backing Up in the Field

Another major concern for photographers shooting on long trips is backing up images in the field. A dreaded scenario is your images are corrupted, or even worse, you lose the flash card with your best shots. Backing up images is very important to making sure your images are safe until you retur n to the office (**FIGURE 2.4**).

I always have my images stored in two places when I am in the field. This way, if one image backup is damaged or lost, I have my images in a second location. There are a variety of options for storing your images in the field.

One source of image backup is flash cards. Flash card prices have dropped, which makes using them for storage a realistic method. I have close to 200 GB of flash cards I can carry in the field. I may shoot 120 GB of images on a long trip, and still have plenty of flash cards to use. I keep my images on the cards I have already shot, just like they were rolls of film. I use flash cards by SanDisk, which are very reliable and have image recovery software if I need it (which I never have).

Portable drives

With my images stored on my flash cards, I still need to back them up in a second place for safe storage. There are three options for this: a portable storage device, a laptop, or external hard drives.

Portable storage devices are units that allow you to download your images directly to the hard drive without the need of a computer. Devices like the Epson P7000 and MemoryKick Si hold gigabytes of images, and allow you to review images on an LCD screen. A real advantage of a portable storage device is its small size and weight. You can easily pack one of these devices in your backpack (**FIGURE 2.5**).

2.4 Backing up images in the field "office."

2.5 A portable storage device allows backup and image review in the field.

2.6 Studio flash packs and battery information ready for travel.

Another option is using your laptop. Laptops give you lots of hard drive space to store images, and all the functionality of a computer in the field. You can work on images at night and post shots to a website when you have Internet access. Some laptops are very small and cost about the same as a portable storage device. The downside is that laptops are not as durable in the field, and more likely to be stolen out of your hotel room when traveling.

External hard drives offer another source of image backup. On many assignments, I download images to my laptop at night, and also download to external hard drives attached to my laptop. These small hard drives are the size of a wallet, and I can carry all my backed-up images with me wherever I go. Some of these drives are also impact- and water-resistant.

In the end, you need to decide where your "image backup comfort level" is. Some photographers back up to three or more places in the field. Backing up to two different locations has never failed me so far.

Navigating Airports and Customs

Another logistical hurdle for photographers is traveling by plane, both domestically and abroad. In Chapter 1, "Pack the Right Gear," we looked at how to pack your camera gear for travel. What about dealing with security and customs officials?

The biggest red flag at security screening for photographers is batteries, especially lithium batteries. Whenever possible, I try to bring my batteries as carry-on items. When I go through screening, I can answer any questions that come up. I also have all the battery information from the manufacturer with me for further clarification. I send my studio packs with my checked baggage, and leave battery and IATA (International Air Transport Association) information in the case. Batteries approved for airline travel by the IATA often have a sticker on them confirming this (**FIGURE 2.6**).

Always have a backup plan for gear that doesn't make it to your destination. Stories abound about flash equipment that is not cleared to go through

checked baggage and photographers missing their flights as a result. See if there are rental houses at your destination. Are there other photographers there who might rent you some gear for a shoot? Clients like solutions, not problems, so always think outside of the box when planning a photo shoot.

I was recently in Mongolia teaching a photo workshop, and brought a small Elinchrom Quadra flash pack. I had no problem entering the country, but at departure the security official wouldn't let me take my Quadra on the plane. He didn't speak English, I didn't know Mongolian, and he refused to let me through security. To solve this dilemma, I went back to the airline counter, explained to them I had flown to Mongolia on their plane with no problems, so why couldn't I fly back the same way? The ticket agent walked with me all the way to security and got in a heated exchange with the official. I don't know what was said, but I made it on the plane with my Quadra. Thinking on your feet is your best asset in tough security situations.

Working in different cultures

One of the most exciting things about adventure sports photography is photographing in foreign destinations. Everything seems fresh and exciting. A simple runner on the street takes on a new meaning when a rickshaw passes by in the background. Colors, smells, and scenes stimulate your creative juices. I remember my first assignment in the Bahamas for *Canoe and Kayak* magazine. Paddling in the Caribbean was like floating in a bottle of Bombay Sapphire. The water was so turquoise that everything looked good. I went wild, shooting everything in sight (**FIGURE 2.7**)!

STAYING HEALTHY ABROAD

You need to be at your best to create compelling images. The last thing you want to do is begin a big shoot in a distant country feeling sick. Before any trip abroad, make sure you check with your doctor for required vaccinations. Some vaccinations require weeks to administer all doses, so start this process early. Consider bringing antibiotics, pain medications, and an extensive first-aid kit if you are going into remote areas. Find out the location of the medical facilities closest to your shoot. And consider taking an advanced first-aid course. In remote areas, you may be the "doctor" for days until help arrives.

2.7 Shooting on assignment in the turquoise waters of the Bahamas.

Research the country you will be shooting in before the trip. Working in English-speaking countries close to home will probably be similar to shooting in the U.S. But the farther off the grid you go, the more cultural differences you will encounter. Some people don't mind having their photo taken, but others find it very offensive. Locals may ask you for money to take their photos. If you don't know the native language, try doing simple gestures to convey your interest in photographing the locals. Remember, you are a guest in their country, so be respectful of local customs.

Hiring a local guide is almost a necessity when working abroad. A guide will know the local customs, speak the language, and direct you toward good photo ops. I always try to work with a local guide; they provide invaluable help and have "saved the day" on many of my trips (**FIGURE 2.8**).

Security is another concern when shooting in foreign countries. Some areas have more crime than others. Check the U.S. State Department's website (http://travel.state.gov) for current travel advisories. Use common sense when shooting in urban areas. Maintain a low profile, and don't carry an $8,000 camera rig around your neck. I shoot in cities using my D300s and one zoom lens. This camera looks less expensive than having a D3 around my neck. Less obtrusive cameras also make locals more comfortable when you are photographing them.

Work permits

If you're hiring a model and shooting for publication, chances are you will need a permit. The types of permits you need will depend on the shoot. Shooting on a public street corner in New York requires obtaining a permit, as does shooting in Denali National Park. Give yourself plenty of time. Permits involve lots of paperwork, documentation of your insurance, and weeks to process, depending on the location and size of the shoot (**FIGURE 2.9**).

On the other hand, if you're just out shooting a friend to create some good images, then you shouldn't need a permit. I've had park rangers ask me what my shoot is about, and if I explain to them I am just shooting on spec, they usually

2.8 Working with a local guide in foreign countries allows better photo opportunities. Naadam Festival, Mongolia.

2.9 Permits are required for many shoots. Photographing mountaineering rangers in Denali National Park.

don't mind. I've tried the same tactic when shooting on a city street corner and been told I couldn't shoot anything without a permit. It just depends.

Photographing in foreign countries is a little different. If you're being hired and paid in the U.S. and staying abroad for only a few weeks, then getting a tourist visa should work just fine. If you're staying longer or working for a client in the destination country, you may need a work visa, the idea being that you are potentially competing with local workers or vendors. But if you're hired in the U.S. and doing all your other business activities in the U.S. except for the actual shoot, a tourist visa should work. Use your local guide to help with these sorts of logistics in your destination country. And if you're just shooting on your own time, be a tourist and have fun!

2.10 Model releases allow you to use images for commercial uses.

Model and Liability Releases

Photographing adventure sports always means shooting people doing activities. You might work with a professional athlete, or randomly encounter people doing outdoor activities. If you have any interest in publishing the image, you should get a model release (**FIGURE 2.10**).

Any time your image is used for commercial and advertising purposes, you should have model releases for any people in the image. You don't need a release for noncommercial uses like magazines and newspapers. The courts have ruled that these publications have more value to inform the public than commercial value requiring a release. Journalists shooting for newspapers don't need model releases for this reason. Also, it has long been understood the person needs to be identifiable in the image in order to require a release.

But here is the catch. Whether a model release should be required or not, many clients insist on one to cover their legal standing. Stock agencies always want model releases. Non-released images go into a different collection than those images with releases. Images with releases have much more money-making potential (advertising uses) than non-released images (**FIGURE 2.11**).

2.11 Model-released images have more income potential.

I always try to get a release. If I'm working with an athlete, I have the athlete sign a model release before the shoot begins. If I am photographing people I find in the outdoors, I always ask them if they will sign a release. I often offer a print in exchange for signing the release. Ninety percent of the time, folks are happy to sign a release. And if they don't want to sign, that's fine as well.

I keep model releases in all my camera bags. The American Society of Media Photographers (www.asmp.org) is a great resource for sample business forms, including model releases. Another amazing tool for generating model releases is the Easy Release app for iPhone, iPad, and Android smartphone users (**FIGURE 2.12**). This application allows you to use a release on your phone that can be signed in the field on the shoot. The signed form is emailed directly to you. Better yet, Easy Release comes in numerous languages with more on the way. Very cool!

Liability waivers

Adventure sports often involve risky activities. A simple paddle down an easy river can turn dangerous when you run into a fallen tree in the river. Taking a short fall while rock climbing can cause you to break an ankle. Adventure sports athletes love what they do, and they know some risk is involved with their chosen activity. For some, the risk factor is what draws them to the sport (**FIGURE 2.13**).

Whenever I set up an adventure sports shoot, I try to have the model sign a liability or assumption-of-risk waiver. This form acknowledges that the activity is potentially dangerous and the photographer is not liable if an injury results. Most athletes I work

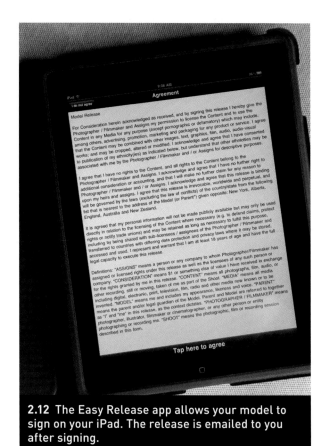

2.12 The Easy Release app allows your model to sign on your iPad. The release is emailed to you after signing.

MODEL RELEASES

- Get a model release if you plan on publishing your images.

- Get a release if you intend to use images of people for advertising and commercial uses.

- Get a release to protect you from claims in the future.

- Find a smartphone application that will give you model releases in many languages; several are available.

with say they would be doing the activity whether I am taking photos or not, because it's what they love to do. My primary goal for any shoot is safety for all those involved, and if I think someone is doing something beyond their ability, I won't do the shoot. Let your models suggest photo ideas; they know their abilities, limitations, and home turf. Don't ask athletes to do routes, jumps, and rivers that they're not comfortable doing just to help you get a shot.

The Planning Checklist

As organized as I like to think I am, I find that having a photo gear checklist keeps me organized for a big trip. This list covers everything related to the photography element of the trip—not just camera gear. A checklist gives me a handy visual inventory of what gear is packed into all those bags and cases. Once something gets packed, it gets checked off the list. This list can be used for any length of trip, from a weekend outing to a month-long expedition (**FIGURE 2.14**).

2.14 Use a gear checklist to ensure you don't forget something. Packing for a canoe trip through Canyonlands National Park.

My Typical Photo Gear Checklist

Some of the items listed here you may not have, and some won't be required on every photography trip. But another benefit of a list such as this is it may give you new ideas on what and how to shoot on your trip. Kiss your habit of forgetting items goodbye!

CAMERA GEAR

- Nikon D3, D300s bodies
- Nikon P7000 (pocket camera)
- 10.5mm fisheye lens
- 14–24mm wide angle lens
- 24–70mm zoom
- 45mm tilt-shift lens
- 70–200mm telephoto zoom
- 1.4x teleconverter
- Gitzo tripod/head
- 160 GB of flash cards
- Polarizer, Grad ND (neutral density) and Vari ND filters
- 2–5 SB900 speedlights
- 1 SU800 transmitter
- 2 SC-29 cords

UNDERWATER CAMERA GEAR

- Aquatech D300s camera housing
- Aquatech fisheye lens port
- Aquatech 24–70mm lens port
- Aquatech SB900 housing
- Housing flash cable
- O-Ring lubricant
- Extra O-Rings

BACKUP DATA STORAGE

- Portable storage device: Epson P7000
- MacBook laptop computer with 250 GB HDD
- Two 500 GB external hard drives

DOCUMENTS

- Visas (if needed)
- Passport (if needed)
- Model releases
- Liability waivers
- Permits
- Immunizations

STUDIO FLASH EQUIPMENT

- 2–5 Elinchrom Rangers or Quadras
- 2–6 flash heads
- Reflectors
- Selection of grids
- Selection of softboxes
- Skyport wireless transmitters/hard cable backups
- 2–6 light stands
- Colored gels

BATTERIES

- Extra camera batteries
- Battery chargers
- AC plug adapters
- AC transformer (if needed)
- Brunton 4.5 solar rolls/cables
- Sustain solar rechargeable battery for cell phone/laptop

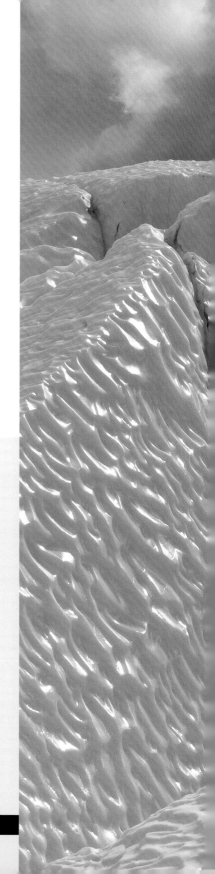

Creative Composition

Good photography combines two elements: technical expertise and artistic vision. Every photographer has a mix of these elements. Without one or the other your photos would suffer. Imagine photographing a kayaker paddling off a 70-foot waterfall. You need to know how fast your shutter speed should be, what aperture will give you sufficient depth of field, and how to set the maximum shooting frame rate on your camera. These are technical aspects of the shoot, and have to be properly set or you will miss some images.

Colby Coombs climbing an ice ridge on the Matanuska Glacier, Alaska.

On the other hand, how are you going to compose the kayaker and waterfall? Are you going to shoot wide to capture more of the environment, or tight to show the gripping details? Where is the kayaker going to be in the frame? Are you going to shoot vertical or horizontal? These are compositional questions that are also critical for the image to succeed.

3.1 A fresh view of hiking in the desert.

There is a photography myth that creativity can't be learned. This is not true. Sure, some people are inherently more creative than others. But this doesn't mean you can't learn creative skills and foster your own vision. Learning composition and developing creativity is like learning a new language. Some people pick up a new language very quickly. Not me—I had to live in Central America for months and study all day to learn Spanish. As with any skill, you need to learn the elements that are fundamental for success, and practice these skills repeatedly to improve. As a photographer, you need to learn to express yourself in a visual medium and improve your visual literacy (**FIGURE 3.1**).

Elements of Design

Good composition begins with understanding the elements of design. *Line, shape, form, texture, pattern,* and *color* are the building blocks of composition. Understanding how these elements work in an image, and how they affect a viewer, is the first step in improving your visual literacy.

Line

Line is the foundation for many design elements, and something all photographers should consider in their images. Lines come in many different forms. Horizontal lines suggest stability, tranquility, and an absence of motion. If you're photographing a warm, idyllic sunset in Maui, the horizontal line at the horizon will help convey this message to the viewer. Vertical lines are also stable, but more dynamic than

3.2 Mountain biking on the White Rim Trail in Canyonlands National Park.

horizontal lines. Lines become more dynamic and suggest motion when they are diagonal—especially jagged diagonal lines. Think of a lightning bolt hitting a mountain summit during a thunderstorm. There is nothing calm or tranquil about this scene, and the lightning bolt further reinforces this concept. Curving lines also imply motion, but in an orderly, calm direction. A mountain biker riding down a winding trail is a good example (**FIGURE 3.2**).

I like to think of lines as *visual handrails*. Lines give the eye a pathway to follow through an image. You can direct the viewer right to your subject using a line. Imagine photographing hikers on a trail. The trail is a perfect

3.3 Watching caribou in the Brooks Range. Note how the gesture of the hiker in the purple shirt creates implied line in the image.

element to connect the foreground, middle ground, and background all together, and lead the viewer straight to the hikers. Without the trail, the eye must roam through the image until the hikers are found. This may work fine, but some viewers may "flip the page" since the hikers aren't obvious.

Another type of line that is important in photography is *implied line*. Implied line is the line that is implied by a gesture or movement, but isn't an actual physical line (**FIGURE 3.3**). When a subject is looking in a particular direction in an image, the viewer naturally looks in the direction the subject is looking. What is he looking at? This is called implied line. If a person is pointing in an image, an implied line is created in the direction he is pointing. It's important to remember not to put your subject on the side of the photo looking out of the image. The viewer will do the same thing: look right out of the picture.

Shape

When a line closes back on itself, it forms a shape. Shape is another design element that conveys different meanings to the viewer. A circle is an eco-friendly shape, often used to imply harmony with the environment. Many native cultures built their shelters in round shapes suggestive of living in harmony with the environment. Adventure sports photography often incorporates two powerful circles in nature: the sun and moon.

Triangles, by contrast, represent power and dominance. How many corporate logos can you think of that use a triangle? A classic mountaineering image shows a small climber with a huge mountain towering overhead. The triangle shape of a mountain helps convey the enormity and dominance of the peak, a great illustration of humans versus nature. Will the climber be successful in a first ascent of this towering peak?

Squares and rectangles convey the human world since they are not common in nature. Imagine a runner jogging down a street lined by houses and buildings. The urban feel is emphasized by the square shapes. The human shape is also very powerful. We can all relate to this shape; it lends perspective and scale to a shot. I often add people in my landscape photographs to humanize the shot and add scale to the image (**FIGURE 3.4**).

Form

Shape is two-dimensional. When shape has three dimensions, it becomes form. Photographing a cliff face straight on shows the shape of the face, but when side lighting casts shadows on the cliff, a form is produced. Whatever the underlying shape conveys compositionally, the form version will reinforce it. A triangle-shaped mountain shown two-dimensionally conveys power. A triangle form conveys power even more (**FIGURE 3.5**).

Form brings up an important shooting concept. By simply changing your perspective, and capturing the same landscape as a different form, you can dramatically change what your image conveys. Try moving a few feet to the left or right and you might improve your image. Or you may need to photograph from the next ridge over. Never get lead feet! Change your shooting position frequently and explore all angles.

Texture

Texture stimulates our sense of touch. I always look for backgrounds or subjects that bring texture into an image. Texture adds flavor and richness to a shot, and can dramatically improve an image. What would you do if you were assigned to photograph a boxer? You could photograph him standing in the street, adding a little sense of where he has come from in his career. But how about putting him in an alley between two brick buildings? The brick walls will add a lot of gritty texture, perfect for conveying the tough survival mentality of being a boxer.

STUDY THE MASTERS

Some days the weather is rainy and gloomy, making it a bad day for going up into the mountains to shoot. These days are perfect for going to your local library and studying design and art. Hundreds of years ago the painting masters were using these same design concepts in their work. Study the art of Monet, Picasso, and Rembrandt. Look at their use of light and design in their paintings.

Studying the work of others will refine your sense of design, and stimulate creativity in your own work. When you do this, you aren't copying the work of others; you are using it as a stepping stone in developing your own photographic style.

3.4 Roping up below the Exit Glacier in Alaska. The size of the human subject in the image leaves little doubt about the size of the glacier.

3.5 Kayaks on the beach surrounded by icebergs, Prince William Sound, Alaska.

3.6 Hiking in Great Sand Dunes National Park, Colorado, against the grainy background of the dunes.

Texture is best captured with side lighting. I photograph a lot in Colorado National Sand Dunes National Park. The dunes are a perfect backdrop for shooting hikers and trail runners. At midday the dunes are interesting, but they transform as the sun starts to set. All the various ridges and ripples start to cast shadows and reveal the grainy texture of the dunes (**FIGURE 3.6**).

Pattern

Pattern is a design element that repeats itself. Pattern can be comprised of any repeating line, shape, form, and so on. Whatever the original element conveyed, a pattern using the element will further strengthen its meaning. Patterns are fun elements to use in adventure sports photography, and are subjects themselves. Sea kayaks in the water create a pleasing pattern of colorful shapes and lines. The shot is about the pattern, not the kayaks, and adds a different perspective to typical kayak images (**FIGURE 3.7**).

3.7 Sea kayaks tied off on the dock, Valdez, Alaska. This image illustrates pattern well.

3.8 Admiring the midnight sun on a mountain bike ride in Alaska. Color attracts the viewer and adds emotion to the shot.

Color

Color, or the absence of color, can define a photographer's career. Color is very powerful in design, and can overpower other design elements. Color has many meanings and social values. White will signify purity and innocence in one culture, and have a very different meaning in another culture. Official colors such as the colors of a country's flag will also convey strong, but different, meanings to viewers depending on their background. Colors also signify emotion. We've all heard the phrase "She's feeling blue" or "He is green with envy."

In a traditional sense, colors convey similar meanings to most people. Painters, like photographers, use this knowledge to create mood and feeling in their paintings. Red signifies danger, love, and heat, and catches the viewer's eye (**FIGURE 3.8**). Red is a very popular color in adventure sports photography because it works well for illustrating high-adrenaline activities. Orange and yellow also attract the viewer's attention, but are friendlier and more inviting.

Blue is a cool, calming color, and has the opposite effect of red. If you want to convey the cold nature of a glacier, include blue fins of ice to reinforce this feeling. Don't warm up the white balance; glaciers are supposed to be cold. Green also has a calming effect, but is really used to illustrate eco-friendly concepts and good health.

Complementary colors are colors that are opposite one another on the color wheel and have a special relationship. When these colors are used side by side in an image, it makes the colors more vibrant. Have you ever wondered why everything looks so good shooting in Arches National Park on a blue-sky day? It's because you are shooting in a complementary color environment (**FIGURE 3.9**).

Absence of color, or black and white, removes much of our color bias from an image, resulting in a raw, pure shot. Portraits and landscape images can be very powerful as black-and-white images. If you

shoot the original image in color and convert it to black and white in the computer, you can have both versions to use.

COMPLEMENTARY COLOR PATTERNS

Use these colors side by side for more vibrant shots:

- Red and green
- Blue and orange
- Yellow and purple

3.9 Complementary colors add punch to your shot.

It's All About Light

Light can make or break your image. A boring subject can look incredible in dramatic light, while a stunning subject can appear mediocre in bad light. Remember this great photo adage: "You are not photographing the subject; you are photographing the light on the subject."

Light should be the number-one thing on your mind when you go out to shoot. What is the light outside? Cloudy or sunny, warm or cool? If the available light isn't working for the shoot, can you use strobe and create your own light to improve the shot?

Qualities of light

Light has three aspects every photographer should consider when shooting: direction, quality, and color.

Direction

The direction from which light hits your subject can dramatically change the mood of your image. Front lighting is the safest, most commonly used direction of light. Well-illuminated subjects generally look good and the colors will pop. Shadows are minimal, and exposure is straightforward (**FIGURE 3.10**).

Side lighting creates shadow, and adds new dimensions to an image; as a result, the image appears more three-dimensional. Side lighting can come from a variety of angles to create varying shadows. Side lighting also often adds mood and drama to a shot.

Backlighting is the least-used type of lighting, and often requires exposure compensation. The subject will be in shadow, requiring you to let in more light to expose properly for the subject. Backlighting works great on translucent subjects and adds dramatic rim light in portraits.

Quality

Light quality refers to the directional quality of light, and can be broken down into two types: non-diffused and diffused light sources. Direct overhead sunlight is non-diffused, high-contrast, and harsh. Shadows are obvious in non-diffused light sources.

3.10 Front lighting illuminates the subject evenly and produces minimal shadows, as reflected in this snowshoeing shot taken in the Colorado high country.

3.11 Side lighting works well for portraits on sunny days.

By contrast, diffused light on a cloudy day produces minimal shadows, and colors saturate nicely. What type of light works best depends on what you are trying to do in your image. Portraits can look flat on overcast days, but your subject won't have to squint. Portraits can also work well in strong sunlight; the trick is photographing your subject so the sun isn't directly in their eyes. Try using side lighting or backlighting to avoid this problem (**FIGURE 3.11**).

Color

The color of the light in your shot is also important, and relates back to what we discussed about color in elements of design. Most people like warm, orange tones since they are inviting and soothing. This is why many photographers prefer to shoot early or late in the day. The sun is warm and rich, bathing subjects in flattering light. Midday light is blue, which is not as inviting, but it can still work for many images. I really like shooting mountain biking in the middle of a sunny day. Nothing says "bluebird day" like a mountain biker on single track in the high country with a sunny blue sky overhead.

USE YOUR INTUITION

When you're first learning composition, it's easy to simply follow the rules. Find the right color; use the best light. But photography situations are very fluid. Every assignment I have ever done had something unexpected happen, sometimes resulting in a great photo. Composition guidelines are a handy tool to use, but stay in touch with your photo intuition during a shoot. Your model may do something unexpected, or the weather may change, and you could be presented with a fantastic photo opportunity. Stay aware of the situation and get the shot.

Viewing an Image

Have you ever stopped to wonder how someone views your image? Not just the casual glance, but how their eye is actually moving through the shot, and what it is relaying to the brain. If we knew this, photographers could conquer the world! Well, not exactly, but we could certainly convey our message more effectively in our work.

One part of visual communication is using your knowledge of design, as mentioned above. Another part is knowing how the viewer will move through your shot. The eye generally follows a few simple principles. First, the viewer will be attracted to bright areas of an image before the dark areas. Bright areas advance, catching the viewer's attention. Put your subject in the light if you want people to see it in your shot. Adding vignettes, or darkening the corners, also directs the viewer to your lit subject. Using flash is all about adding light where you want to direct the viewer's attention. Similarly, strong saturated colors also attract the viewer to an area in the image.

Next, most people like order and simplicity in images. Busy, blurry shots are are unattractive and hard to figure out. The eye will go to sharp, in-focus areas before it goes to out-of-focus areas. Using shallow depth of field works great for this. The background goes soft and out of focus, allowing the tack-sharp subject to jump off the background.

High-contrast areas in a given scene will attract attention before the low-contrast areas. I often add a rim light illuminating the shoulders of a subject in a portrait. This rim light will add separation of the subject from the background and make the subject stand out. Look for scenes in the outdoors that give you the same effect. Hikers walking on a sunlit ridge with a shaded mountain behind them will create natural high contrast in the shot and catch people's attention (**FIGURE 3.12**).

3.12 High-contrast subjects will get the viewer's attention, as in this shot of hikers in Alaska's Talkeetna Mountains.

Rule of Thirds

Another technique that helps create compelling images is *the rule of thirds*. This rule states that by putting the subject in certain areas of a rectangular frame results in natural, pleasing locations for the subject. Think of your camera's viewfinder, but with lines crossing it in a checkerboard pattern (many cameras have a grid viewfinder showing these lines). Where these lines intersect are natural sweet spots of the image, and good places to put your subject.

The rule of thirds works for both vertical and horizontal compositions. I often try to photograph my subject in a variety of these locations for different perspectives. If the subject is moving in a particular direction (or looking one way), I will place them with more negative space in the direction they are moving.

Perspective

One of the most exciting things about photography is getting your images back. It's like opening presents on Christmas morning. And the most rewarding moment is seeing your original idea and angle come to life.

When I teach photo workshops, one point I try to get across is that everyone has their own perspective. I'm amazed at how many different images can be produced of the same scene by a row of photographers all shooting in the same place. The downfall is when you get complacent standing behind your tripod and don't work a scene to its full potential. You may get one good image, but what about the other shots you missed (**FIGURE 3.13**)?

Early in my photography career when I was assisting in a studio, a photographer told me that if I ever found myself standing there holding my camera taking a picture of a scene, I was doing something wrong. Every photographer can stand there with a camera, point, and shoot. How many images do you have in your files that you shot using this exact method? The bigger question is not can you capture the scene but, rather, what can you bring to a shot that others don't see or aren't able to do? If you photograph rock climbers, chances are you'll need to ascend a rope to photograph them from above. This technical ability will set you apart from many other photographers. Maybe once you're on a rope dangling above the climber you can add some flash. This technique will separate you from even more climbing photographers, and your image will be unique. Finally, you build a tripod that pushes you away from the vertical rock face for a new, original perspective. What you've done through these steps is come up with a unique perspective, and develop a style of shooting that separates you from the masses.

I really like to stop and think about what I'm trying to accomplish when I consider perspective. Am I trying to show how high a boulder problem is, or how difficult the route is? A low angle will add size and scale to the shot, while a tight angle on the climber's hand will convey the dicey nature of the route. Really think about what you're trying to accomplish, then choose the angle and perspective that best illustrate this concept. Get down low, climb a ladder, push your lens against a tree trunk. Try everything you can think of for a shot, this is your moment to let your creativity shine!

3.13 Too close for comfort on the Matanuska Glacier. Look for original perspectives to catch the viewer's attention.

Capturing emotion

Some concepts are fairly straightforward to capture in an image. If you set out to capture pattern, any repeating shape should work just fine. This is a very tangible concept. But what if your assignment is to capture mood and emotion? And to make it more challenging, you can't photograph people or animals. Now your mind is spinning in creative ways because there isn't an obvious answer. Creative thinking is good!

Capturing emotion involves using your knowledge of design and finding the right moment. Imagine a kayaker paddling through a tough rapid. The kayaker's boat is a bright color that catches the viewer's attention. The wave crests create a series of jagged, diagonal lines, also perfect for implying dramatic motion. You zoom in on his face and see the determination as he crashes through the waves. This image of his expression, along with other design elements, conveys emotion in the final shot. The casual observer viewing this image in a gallery is going to get sweaty palms looking at this kayaker (**FIGURE 3.14**).

If you want people to have strong responses to your images, capturing emotion and drama will help. Photograph your outdoor athletes with an awareness of moments that show emotion. Accomplishing a new route, winning a race, or getting stuck in a storm are ripe scenarios for capturing emotion. Observers will empathize with subjects showing strong emotion.

I often do self-assignments, which are great for stirring your creative juices. Creativity is like any activity: You have to continually practice, practice, practice to get better. Assign yourself a photo essay of your favorite adventure sport, and make sure to add capturing emotion in the mix. This will force you to look at things differently, and broaden your creativity in your coverage of the activity.

Developing your style

Now that you have a taste of composition and creativity, it's time to put it all together. Since most of us are shooting digitally, there are no film and developing costs to worry about. Experiment with your ideas and try new things. The way to grow creatively and technically as a photographer is by making a lot of mistakes.

One thing I have learned after shooting for a long time is that *the process is important as the end result.* I have done countless shoots trying something new and produced zero decent images as a result. Early in my career this caused a lot of frustration. But I began to realize that even though I didn't get the image I wanted, I had learned something new. I wouldn't make the same mistake again, and sometimes I even learned something I had no idea would be the outcome (**FIGURE 3.15**).

Rules are made to be broken. I have listed a number of composition guidelines in this chapter, and that is exactly what they are—guidelines. These principles will help with your composition, but they are not the final answer. Break the rules, put subjects where you wouldn't normally place them, try radical, slanted

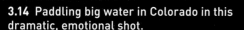

3.14 Paddling big water in Colorado in this dramatic, emotional shot.

3.15 Experiment and try new techniques to develop your style. Here's a fly-fishing shot taken with a tilt-shift lens to exaggerate selective focus.

angles. The worst that can happen is your finger gets sore hitting the trash-can icon on the back of your camera.

As you grow as a photographer, you will capture images similar to those that others have taken, and hopefully go beyond them. Having a unique style is very important for the working photographer. Your style is what sets you apart from other photographers, and why a client will hire you over another photographer.

Finding your photographic style can be elusive. It's like searching for an intangible object that's hard to grasp. Instead of searching for your style, your style will find you. As you experiment and grow creatively, your photographic style will emerge. And through the years, your style will continue to evolve and change.

WHAT IS YOUR STYLE?

Try this exercise to identify your strengths and weaknesses as a photographer, and what your shooting style is. Pick 40 of your best images, and view them as a contact sheet on your computer. Ask these questions about the images: Are they color or black and white? Are they vertical or horizontal? Are they tight shots or wide angle? What lens did you use the most? What aperture? Are there people in the images? What activities were you capturing? Do any of the images use flash?

Answering these questions will identify your shooting preferences and strengths. These images represent your style. This is a good thing. Now you know what you can do well, and what areas need work to develop your photography skills.

To grow and evolve as a photographer, you need to "shoot outside the box." It's time to experiment and make some mistakes. Put away your favorite telephoto lens and shoot all day with a wide-angle lens. You'll be frustrated, but this exercise will force you to see in a different way. And down the road, your vision and creativity will be greater.

Ten Composition Tips

Wouldn't it be great if there were a list of "Ten steps to creative enlightenment"? Well, now there is! Below is a list of ten tips that will help you develop your creativity and create dynamic compositions. Try these out on your next shoot. And remember, as artists we are never satisfied with our work. Photography is a journey with highs (good images) and lows (trash-can shots). We are always trying to satisfy our creative urge through creating photographs representing our vision.

1. **Use one lens all day.** If you like to shoot with a telephoto, then use a 24mm wide angle all day. Don't cheat by using a super zoom—it won't help! Forcing yourself to use an unlikely lens for a subject will get you seeing things differently.

2. **Shoot at your home.** As we become familiar with our surroundings, our creativity is dimmed and we "put the blinders on." We stop seeing the world from a graphic standpoint; subjects become familiar. Try creating a photo essay of your home and yard. You have to get creative to make interesting photographs out of familiar everyday objects!

3. **Get really close.** On your next portrait shoot, try getting really close to your subject. This may make you uncomfortable, but that's the point! You'll have to interact at a new level with your subject, and the images you produce will reflect the connection you make.

4. **Photograph the stars.** Photographing stars accomplishes a number of things. It forces you to shoot at night, a time most photographers aren't out. And you'll need to learn how to take long exposures, good for refining photo technique.

5. **Use flash.** Many photographers are intimidated by using flash, which limits their ability to photograph certain situations. If you never use flash, start learning how to use simple fill flash. If you're a flash master, then experiment with a new lighting technique.

6. **Focus on color.** Color is a very powerful design element. Work on self-assignments focused on color as the subject. Create images where color supports the concept and photograph complementary color patterns (**FIGURE 3.16**).

7. **Shake your camera.** Do you ever get tired of shooting the same subject over and over? Next time you're shooting that same subject, try shaking the camera during the exposure. You'll create some wild abstracts, and may get some new ideas to use on future shoots.

8. **Take an implied portrait.** Here is a challenge: Try to take a portrait without the actual physical subject in the photo. How is that possible? There are many ways to do it. Turn on your creative right brain and figure it out!

9. **Read your camera manual.** For some photographers, myself included, this is like pulling teeth. But you might just learn something you didn't know, such as how take time-lapse images, or how to select the number of focus points being used.

10. **Practice, practice, practice.** The worst thing you can do as a photographer is stop taking photos. To improve, you need to keep shooting. Take that camera out and shoot a few pics of any subject. Going through the motions will keep your technique and creativity sharp.

3.16 Try using complementary colors and motion blur for a new look. Mountain biking at Hatcher Pass, Alaska.

Lighting in the Field

Lighting is key to the success of any image. Without light, there would be no photographs. My life revolves around light. I wake up early for it. I plan vacations around it. I buy special gear to capture it. My career depends on it. Photographers are joined at the hip with light.

Adventure sports photography relies on good light to make compelling images. Photographing mountaineers on a glacier on an overcast day is like shooting flies in pea soup. Everything is flat and murky with no contrast. The viewer can't see any detail in the snow; it's a featureless, foggy mess. If the climbers are wearing drab clothes, they look like brown boulders in a snowfield. Not good.

Using flash on this wake surfer adds drama and tension to the image.

But then the sun comes out, and this mountaineering scene is transformed. Detail emerges in the snow, and steep ridges and deep crevasses are revealed. The climber's Gortex jacket brightens, and his skin tones rosy up. Nature just turned on the light switch.

I speak from experience. Once I shot a new clothing line for Columbia Sportswear in Alaska. We had decided mountaineering would be a great way to illustrate what the new clothes could do. I had hired climbers to be the models since they would actually be climbing in serious situations. The climbers had climbed up a ridge for a shot, and I had set up a quarter-mile away with a telephoto lens to compress the scene. There was no scene; only dull shapes on featureless white. I was sweating bullets since the shoot depended on good light. But then the sun broke through a hole in the clouds and perfectly illuminated the climbers. I squeezed off a few shots, and then the clouds pinched the sun out. But I had my shot (**FIGURE 4.1**).

4.1 Climbers roping up on a ridge on the Matanuska Glacier, Alaska.

Natural Light

Natural light has been the mainstay of adventure sports photography for years. Adventure sports take place outdoors, so the easiest and most logical source to use is available light. And the good news is, natural light creates stunning images. If you use the lighting and design principles outlined in Chapter 3, "Creative Composition," your images should look good. Seek out warm light for pleasing landscapes. Look for edgy light situations. Put your model in the sun with a dark-shadowed background and you should have a dramatic image. On overcast days use a slower shutter speed (since there is less light) to create pan-and-blur images (Chapter 6, "Photographing Water Sports").

Every time I head out the door on a photo shoot, the first thing I do is evaluate the light (**FIGURE 4.2**). What I see determines how I will proceed on a shoot. If it's sunny, figures in a landscape with lots of blue sky will work great. If it's overcast with pasty-white skies, I'll focus on smaller scenes or shoot in the forest. And I have another option with natural light: I can alter the direction and quality of available light using light modifiers.

4.2 A photographer's day begins with evaluating the light.

Reflectors

Reflectors are light modifiers that reflect light on to a subject. Generally, we think of specialty reflectors designed for photographers, but natural reflectors are abundant in the field. Snowfields and sandy beaches reflect a lot of light onto subjects. Water reflects sunlight into a kayaker's face. Always be aware of natural reflectors you can use in your image (**FIGURE 4.3**).

Light reflected back on your subject will fill in shadows and reduce contrast. Reflected light also reflects color onto your subject. If you use a white reflector, it will reflect white light on the subject. If the reflector is gold, then the light will have an orange color.

One important characteristic of a reflector is its *throw,* or the distance it can reflect light back into a scene. Silver reflects light the most efficiently, and

LUCK FAVORS THE PREPARED

Sometimes during photo workshops, a participant asks me what separates the pro photographer from the amateur. Invariably I reply, "The pro photographer takes more pictures." Of course, this isn't the whole story—most pros have advanced technique and a strong style. But there is truth in this statement. If you want to take good photographs, you have to get out and shoot. Images aren't made sipping coffee on a rainy day at the café; they're made out in the rain. The more you shoot, the better your chances of creating a good image and improving your technique. Sometimes, a viewer will tell me how lucky I was to get a shot. Luck is certainly a part of the equation, but you have to be out shooting in the field to be lucky. So get that camera and go out and shoot!

4.3 Sand and water are natural reflectors that can be used in adventure photography.

can reflect light into a scene from a long way away. This works great when you are photographing a large scene and want to add some reflected light into the scene. The person holding the silver reflector can be outside the field of view and still reflect light onto the subject.

Reflectors come in a variety of shapes, sizes, and colors. Collapsible reflectors work great for adventure sports photography. Small sizes collapse down to round disks about a foot in diameter, yet expand

big enough to reflect light for portraits. I like to use Lastolite TriGrips. These reflectors have a handle that makes holding and positioning them much easier, especially in the wind. My TriGrip has a variety of interchangeable fabric colors that slip onto the reflector. I use soft gold, white, and silver the most (**FIGURE 4.4**).

Larger reflectors are also a good choice for adventure sports shooting, but they're better used closer to the car since they're bigger and heavier. I use

42" × 78" and 78" × 78" Lastolite Skylite reflectors for big light jobs. These reflectors have a metal frame with material attached via Velcro and reflect a large amount of light into a scene. Often I use the Skylite with white material to reflect light back into scenes.

An advantage of using reflectors is that the reflected light is easier to meter and preview on the scene. You can see what the reflected light looks like, and meter accordingly. With flash you get a quick burst of light that can be harder to visualize.

Using a reflector is simple: Just position the reflector to aim sunlight or another light source back onto your subject. To control the intensity of the light, move backward or forward from your subject. A big mistake that photographers often make when using reflectors is getting really close to their subject and overpowering them with light. If you reflect full sunlight onto your subject from a foot away using a gold reflector, your model will look like a sunburned tourist in Cabo. Back away to get less powerful reflected light. And when you're not shooting photographs, make sure to lower the reflector to ease the strain on your model's eyes (**FIGURE 4.5**).

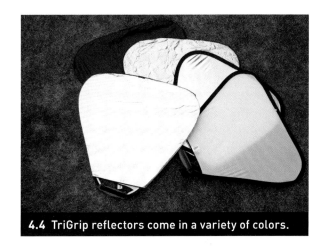

4.4 TriGrip reflectors come in a variety of colors.

REFLECTOR TIPS

- Choose the color you want to reflect. White and soft gold work best.

- Use black reflectors to subtract light and add contrast.

- Control light output by moving the reflector closer to or farther from your subject.

- Position the reflector far enough from your subjects so you don't overpower them.

4.5 A reflector is used to reflect light back onto the subject.

Overhead silks

Another way to control and modify natural light is using an overhead silk. Overhead silks are large white panels that allow light through in varying intensities. Some silks reduce light by 1 stop, others by 2 stops. As with reflectors, they come in a variety of sizes, from small handheld reflectors to large overhead silks (**FIGURE 4.6**).

Overhead silks are portable shade producers, and a great item to have for shooting portraits on a bright, sunny day. If there is no shade around, you can position your model under a silk and get great, smooth, wraparound light. You can also use other reflectors and strobes with overhead silks and create nice lighting for portraits.

Start by using an overhead silk to soften the light on your subject. Then use a soft gold reflector to reflect light onto one side of your subject, creating

4.6 Using an overhead silk for a portrait.

some contrast and interesting light for your shot. To increase shadows on the opposite side, use a black reflector to subtract light. Using the sun as your main light and modifying it with reflectors and overhead silks, you can create terrific portraits using available light.

Artificial Light

Let's face it. All adventure photographers dream about golden crepuscular sun bathing their subjects in flattering light. And sometimes that happens. But a lot of times it doesn't. Instead, you're dealt overcast skies and flat light, or midday sun scorching you and your subject. At other times, you're shooting at twilight and need more light. Don't despair, because artificial light offers lots of solutions.

Why use flash in the first place? Many outdoor photographers are cautious using flash because it looks unnatural. This is a legitimate concern, and you (or your client) must be happy with the final image. But using flash effectively is a great photographic tool. Flash adds highlights to an image and directs the viewer to this part of the shot. Flash will add contrast, produce creative shadows, fill in shadows, punch up color, add catch lights in the eyes, brighten overall exposure, add motion streaks ... the list is long. If any of these aspects are important in the shot you're trying to capture, then using flash may be the right approach (**FIGURE 4.7**).

Artificial light saves my photographic day, and makes my images stand out from the pack. When I'm on an assignment, I can't just put my camera away if the light isn't what I want. I need to use my photographic savvy and create my own light. Understanding artificial light technique using speedlights and strobes is crucial for the adventure sports photographer. And today's flash technology is opening up new image possibilities that were impossible just a year ago.

4.7 Using flash punches up color in this image.

Speedlight flash

Flash photography at its most basic begins with on-camera pop-up flashes and speedlights, which are larger flashes that attach to the camera hot shoe. Both of these flash options offer many benefits to adventure sports shooters, including small size, TTL metering, and high-speed sync. If you've been intimidated by flash photography in the past, this is your starting point.

Pop-up flashes are handy because they're an integral part of the camera. You pop them up when you need them, and close them when you don't. Pop-up flashes can add catch light to eyes and fill in shadows under a hat. But pop-up flashes have limited power and can't be used off camera. Speedlights are the next choice. Every adventure sports photographer should have one.

Speedlight flash modes

Speedlights offer many advantages for shooting adventure sports. They are small, operate on AA batteries, and can easily be carried into the field. Another big advantage of speedlights is the compatibility of the flash with your DSLR camera. The flash will work with different metering modes and relay focal-length information. Speedlights have a variety of shooting modes, but there are two in particular that work great in adventure sports photography: TTL and Manual mode.

In TTL mode, speedlights use TTL metering to control the flash output. This means the light is measured *through the lens*, resulting in accurate flash exposures. This approach works very well in fast-moving situations where you don't have time to set up manual flash exposures. Mountain bikers and kayakers don't wait on you and your flash; you need to be able to aim the flash at the subject wherever they are and get a decent exposure. TTL flash does the trick (**FIGURE 4.8**).

Sometimes TTL flash is too powerful in the shot, resulting in "over-flashed" images. Try reducing the flash output 1–2 stops for a more balanced flash/ambient light exposure. Some speedlights offer Balanced Fill Flash mode, which nicely blends flash and ambient light. I use SB900s in Balanced Fill Flash mode for nice fill light and a good background exposure.

Sometimes TTL mode doesn't work well. If you encounter a tricky metering situation, your flash exposure may be off or inconsistent. This is when Manual flash mode is the right choice. Manual flash exposure allows you to set the speedlight output for consistent results, eliminating TTL flash output metering. Most speedlights allow you to adjust the flash output from full power downward in 1/3-stop increments. Once you have your flash power dialed in, you get consistent flash output for each shot (**FIGURE 4.9**).

4.8 Using flash in TTL mode allows you to shoot very quickly in the field.

4.9 Using manual flash mode to ensure consistent flash output on each shot.

LIGHT PAINTING

You don't need flashes to illuminate every scene. Try buying a small flashlight at your local hardware store and light painting a scene. Light painting involves illuminating a dark scene with a continuous source of light such as a flashlight or rechargeable spotlight. Set your exposure to Bulb, your aperture to f/5.6, and your ISO to 200 for a starting exposure. A locking cable release works well to hold the shutter open in Bulb mode. Autofocus doesn't work in the dark, so you'll need to manually focus. Shoot at twilight so the sky will have some color. Any object will work, from small flowers to large desert arches. Add light in small bursts from side angles to create shadow and interesting highlights in the shot. The key is to illuminate certain areas of a scene, not flood the whole shot with light (**FIGURE 4.10**). Experiment with different white balance settings for different looks. Light painting is addictive. Be careful or you will be out all night—not a bad thing!

Triggering flash off camera

Once you've decided what speedlight mode to use, the next question is how to use it effectively. If you attach your speedlight to your camera hot shoe, you're using it in a manner similar to a pop-up flash. You can add some nice fill flash and punch up the colors, and some fast shooting situations are best photographed with on-camera flash. But your creative choices are very limited with the flash on the same axis as the lens. Take your speedlight off camera for some real drama (**FIGURE 4.11**).

Using your speedlight off camera will give you many more options to modify the light. One huge advantage is that you can create shadow and contrast by shooting the flash at an angle to your subject. You can transform a two-dimensional scene into a three-dimensional scene. Simply put, using your speedlight off camera is one of the best ways to improve your flash photography.

4.10 Light painting involves using a flashlight to add light to a scene.

4.11 Using a speedlight off camera allows creative lighting angles and gives you the ability to create shadow.

BOUNCE FLASH

Bounce flash can simulate off-camera flash but uses the flash on camera. Speedlights have an adjustable flash head that can be aimed at a surface to bounce light back onto a subject. The most common scenario is bouncing light off a white ceiling to illuminate a subject. Instead of the light hitting the subject straight on from on-camera flash, the light bounces off the ceiling and hits the subject from above. You can also bounce light off a wall to create side lighting on a subject. An important point to remember is bounce flash will produce light with the color of the bounce surface. White walls are great. Green walls produce alien portraits.

You don't need to be inside to use bounce flash. Frequently, I bounce flash off reflectors to add soft, diffused light to my subject. Bouncing flash off a soft gold reflector produces a nice, warm light for a portrait.

There are many options to trigger your flash off camera. Almost every flash can be used off camera using a dedicated cable between the speedlight and camera hot shoe. These cables allow full control of all the speedlight's functions just as if they were attached to the camera. I use SC-29 cables to trigger my SB900s. These 9-foot cables can be tethered together for more length. Cables are inexpensive, reliable, and the easiest way to use your flash off camera. The downside is the cable limits the range of where you can use your speedlight. For even more flexibility, I use a wireless transmitter.

Wireless transmitters relay flash information from the camera to a flash with a wireless receiver. Many camera systems have a dedicated wireless system where the speedlights have a receiver built in—all you need is the transmitter. I use a Nikon SU-800 transmitter to trigger my SB 900s wirelessly. The SU-800 uses an optical signal to control three separate groups of flashes. Flashes can be used in many modes including TTL mode, and output is controlled at the camera from the SU-800. This is very handy when you're working alone (**FIGURE 4.12**).

Other wireless systems use a radio signal to control speedlights. Radio wireless systems can trigger speedlights from farther distances and work well in bright sun (sometimes direct sun interferes with optical signals). Pocket

4.12 Using an SU800 wireless transmitter allows control of three different groups of speedlights.

Wizard and Radio Popper systems use radio signals and offer control similar to a dedicated optical system. You need both a transmitter and receiver to use these systems.

Modifying the quality of light

In Chapter 3, we discussed the three important principles of light: direction, quality, and color. Now that you can use flash off camera and control direction, the next consideration is changing the quality of light coming from your flash. You have lots of options.

Many photographers like to use soft, diffused light on their subject. Diffused light is very forgiving, fills in skin imperfections, and gives people a healthy glow. Since the light coming from a speedlight is very directional and harsh, you need to diffuse it to soften the light quality. The easiest way to diffuse a speedlight is to put a diffusion dome on top of the flash. Most flashes come with this dome included. A diffusion dome will spread the light and take the harsh edge off it, which may be all that is needed for some images. But one rule holds true when diffusing your flash. The softness of the light is directly proportional to the size of the light source and how close it is to the subject (**FIGURE 4.13**). Since the diffusion dome is small, it doesn't diffuse the light much, even if it is close to your subject.

There are many small softboxes designed for speedlight use that work well. I use Lastolite Ezyboxes. What I like about these softboxes is they use an inner and outer diffusion layer for very soft light, similar to a studio-sized softbox. The Speed-Lite model attaches directly to your flash using Velcro

straps, and is the smallest of the bunch. This softbox is great when you want to soften the light in fast situations or precarious spots. For more diffusion I use a Lastolite 54 cm Ezybox. This softbox requires a bracket to hold the speedlight, and produces very soft light. I can handhold this softbox while shooting, but it's easier to set it on a stand or have a friend hold it.

4.13 Using a softbox will soften the light on your subject.

4.14 Justin Clamps allow easy speedlight fastening to light stands and anything you can clamp.

Another option for producing soft light is shooting speedlights through diffusion material. Many reflectors have translucent material that will soften flash. You can also shoot multiple speedlights through a larger diffusion panel for a very soft light. I attach my speedlights to the crossbar of my diffusion panel using Manfrotto 175F Justin Clamps. These clamps have a cold-shoe mount to attach your flash, and are very handy for putting flashes on light stands and difficult spots (**FIGURE 4.14**).

What if you don't want to soften the light, but want to focus the area where the light hits? This requires snoots and grids, which are also available for speedlights. I use Rogue Flash Benders to control the angle of light. These units attach to your flash head using Velcro. The snoot has flexible metal bars that allow you to shape the opening from a narrow slit to as wide as your flash head. If I don't want my flash

that narrow, but still want to keep the light from spilling into a scene, I use grids by Honl or Rogue. These grids come in a variety of sizes and are great for controlling light in small spaces.

Changing the color of light

The last aspect of light you can control is the color of light. Heat-resistant acetate, or *gels*, is used to change the color of flash. Some gels color correct light sources to precise color temperatures while other gels add theatrical effects. I use Nikon gels that came with my SB900s. These gels fit in a plastic holder that attaches to the front of the flash. I also use gels by Rosco, a company that offers a wide selection of colors, and has gels sized for speedlights as well as larger studio lights. Gels can be attached using gaffer tape to larger flashes.

My favorite use of a gel is putting a full CTO (orange) on my flash, and setting my camera white balance to incandescent. Incandescent white balance turns daylight blue. Since my flash is approximately daylight in color temperature, the flash would be blue without a gel. But the orange gel will counter the incandescent white balance. Anything the flash hits will be neutral in color. This is a great technique for cloudy skies. The blue color makes the sky moody, and the illuminated subject really stands out in the scene (**FIGURE 4.15**).

High-speed sync

One shooting mode is especially important for the adventure sports photographer: high-speed sync. Since so many of the subjects I photograph are moving, it's very important to be able to freeze the action in a fill flash mode. If the daylight is

4.15 Using an orange gel and setting your camera white balance to incandescent can result in dramatic effects.

4.16 High-speed sync allows you to use fast shutter speeds and flash.

underexposed by 2 stops or more, then the flash duration will freeze the action, not the shutter speed. But if I'm using flash and the daylight exposure isn't underexposed by much, then the shutter speed will stop the action.

High-speed sync allows you to shoot at speeds faster than your normal flash sync speed, generally around 1/250. Using high-speed sync I can shoot at shutter speeds all the way to 1/8000 to freeze any scene I encounter (**FIGURE 4.16**). In high-speed sync mode, speedlights emit a pulsating beam of light to ensure that flash is present no matter how fast the shutter is moving.

High-speed sync also offers another advantage: It allows you to shoot at wide-open apertures in the middle of the day. Imagine attempting to photograph a fly fisherman in the middle of a sunny day and using fill flash. If you choose f/2.8 as your aperture, set your ISO to 100 (the lowest ISO setting on many cameras), you'll need to set your shutter speed around 1/2000 or faster to get the right exposure. High-speed sync will allow you to use flash and this fast shutter speed. Using fast shutter speeds in the middle of the day also lets you underexpose the daylight and create dark, dramatic backgrounds for portraits.

The one limitation of high-speed sync is that your effective flash distance is greatly reduced. To improve the range of speedlights in high-speed sync mode, I use multiple units. I use a Lastolite Triflash bracket to attach three speedlights, which greatly improves the flash range. This bracket can be placed on a light stand or handheld (**FIGURE 4.17**). I often place my Triflash bracket on the pointed end of my ski pole to use as a light stand when I am shooting skiing. I also attach multiple flashes to light stands using Justin Clamps.

Triggering multiple flashes wirelessly in high-speed sync mode is similar to triggering one. I will use my Nikon SU800 to trigger my speedlights when I am working close to my flashes. If I need to trigger my flashes from a distance, then I will use Radio Poppers or the Pocket Wizard Flex system to trigger the flashes. You need to attach a receiver to each flash in order to use all the flashes in high-speed sync mode. Radio poppers have an impressive range; you can trigger flashes around 1/4 of a mile away.

4.17 A Lastolite TriFlash bracket and Radio Poppers increase the range of speedlights.

DON'T LET THE TECHNICAL INHIBIT THE CREATIVE

Learning flash technique can be intimidating at first. Instead of relying on the sun, you're now creating your own light and controlling all aspects of it. When most people are learning flash technique, their creativity goes out the door. Photographers become much more focused on getting the lights set up, figuring out exposure, and setting channels on their wireless transmitter. Meanwhile, your subject has fallen asleep and you've barely considered the creative aspects of the shoot. Practice will reduce the amount of time you spend deciding how to light a subject. Your lights will be ready to go, and you'll be able to connect with your subject and focus on the creative aspects of the shoot.

4.18 Studio strobes allow the use of larger softboxes to project very diffused light on your subject.

Large flash systems

Speedlights are great portable units for shooting adventure sports, but sometimes you need more power and faster recycling times. When I photograph kayakers in the middle of a rapid, I need a very powerful light to reach the kayaker. I could use multiple speedlights, but I'd soon reach the point where using one big light would be more practical than using a bunch of small lights. Large flash systems offer lots of power and the ability to use bigger light modifiers on your shoot (**FIGURE 4.18**).

Functionality in the field

Most of your adventure sports shooting will take place in the backcountry where you won't have AC power close at hand. On my backcountry shoots I use a battery-powered flash system by Elinchrom. I use the 1100-watt Ranger and 400-watt Quadra flash packs. These lights have lots of battery power, quick flash-recycling times, and are very durable in the field. My Ranger pack has survived blizzards, desert heat, and heavy rain, and it's never missed a pop.

4.19 The Elinchrom Skyport system allows flash triggering and power control of the Ranger pack from the camera.

A big advantage of the Elinchrom system is its ability to control flash output from a wireless transmitter attached to your camera. This system, called Skyport, is very handy when you place your flash packs in hard-to-reach spots. I sometimes place a Ranger on the side of the river opposite the one I'm shooting from when I photograph kayakers. Since I can control output at the camera, I don't have to keep crossing the river to adjust my lights (**FIGURE 4.19**).

Pack size is the real concern for the adventure sports shooter. The Ranger packs weigh around 17 pounds, which limits how far you might bring them in the field, but the advantage is all the power you get. The Quadra pack isn't as powerful, but it weighs only about 6 pounds, making it a great choice when weight is a big concern.

Using large flash systems

Large flash systems like the Elinchrom Ranger and Quadra work differently from a speedlight. These flashes work in manual mode; there is no TTL

metering or automatic fill flash. Also, you need to choose what reflector to use with the strobe head for your shoot.

I always start by establishing my ambient, daylight exposure. Sometimes I like the daylight exposure to be right on target, and use my flash to add some fill light to shadow areas in the image. But more often I like to underexpose my daylight exposure 1–2 stops. When I add flash to this underexposed scene, everything the flash illuminates will *pop off the canvas*, creating separation of my subject from the background. Underexposing your background will also add some mood and drama to the image. How you expose the daylight in your shot should relate to what you're trying to create in the final image. Some shots are all about high-key bright scenes and shouldn't be underexposed. Other shots work great with the background underexposed, adding tension to the final image (**FIGURE 4.20**).

After I've established the background exposure, I add flash to the image. I decide what reflector or softbox to use on the head, and how many lights I need for my image. I don't use a light meter since many of my subjects are far away or in precarious positions. I simply trigger the flashes and see how things look on my LCD. I adjust the light output until I get the right exposure. I use my highlight (blinkies) indicator on my LCD screen to help determine my flash exposure. Since I'm using the Skyport wireless system with my flash packs, I can adjust my lights very quickly right at the camera.

Flash heads are bigger than a speedlight, so I use light stands to position my lights. Manfrotto makes a wide variety of stands that will take years of use (or abuse). I use Manfrotto 367B 9-foot stands for most of my shooting. These are light enough to carry into the field, and collapse small enough to fit in a suitcase for travel. If I'm using large softboxes and need a stronger stand, I use the Manfrotto Alu Master 12-foot stand.

A big advantage of using studio lights is the wide variety of light modifiers the flash heads can use. I use many types of softboxes, ranging from square softboxes and strip banks to large octabanks. I will use standard reflectors when I need hard-edged light in a scene (**FIGURE 4.21**). These reflectors also accept grids to help control the spill of light. I also use a sports reflector on my flash head when I need to project my flash as far as I can into a scene.

Ranger high-speed sync

My Elinchrom Ranger syncs at 1/200 of a second. This means that I can't shoot any faster than this or

4.20 Determine your lighting ratio between flash and ambient light to get the effect you want in the final shot.

4.21 Hard-edged light works well to add highlights to an image.

I will clip the flash. Clipped flash appears as a dark band across your image where the shutter clipped part of the flash. Can you freeze action at 1/200? Absolutely, but it is your flash duration, not the shutter speed, that will do the job.

In order to freeze action, you need to reduce or eliminate the daylight in your shot. The daylight exposure is tied directly to the shutter speed, so a fast-moving skier will not look sharp at 1/200. But if you darken the daylight exposure so that the flash is the main light illuminating your subject, then the flash will become the light source that will freeze the subject. My Elinchrom Ranger A-heads have a very fast flash duration—1/2300 and faster—that's more than fast enough to freeze a skier. Always consider the flash duration of the light when you're purchasing a studio flash system.

Can you use high-speed sync with studio lights? Yes, yes, yes! Until recently, studio packs couldn't operate past their maximum sync speed, but with Pocket Wizard's Hypersync technology, you can shoot at shutter speeds of 1/800 and faster. Hypersync is a utility that recalibrates the shutter and flash timing, allowing faster sync speeds. You need one of their MinTT1 or FlexTT5 transmitters and a dedicated receiver for your flash unit. Results will vary depending on your flash system and the camera you are using (**FIGURE 4.22**).

With my Elinchrom Ranger system, I use the S-heads for the best results. These heads have a slower flash duration, which gives Hypersync more latitude to time the shutter and flash. And the results are staggering. I can sync my Nikon D3 around 1/800, much faster than 1/200. With my

4.22 High-speed sync is available using large flash packs. Elinchrom Ranger shot at 1/2500.

D300s, I can sync all the way to 1/8000! I get a tiny bit of flash clipping at this speed, easy to crop out in post-production. And I still get a lot of flash power and distance at this shutter speed. Remember, this high speed is good not only for stopping action, but also for shooting with a wide-open aperture in the middle of the day (**FIGURE 4.23**). The Quadra can also sync faster using Hypersync, a FlexTT5 as a receiver, and an S-head. Since the Quadra has a built-in wireless receiver, the FlexTT5 is plugged into the sync port of the pack.

Effective outdoor flash: Two scenarios

What is the best light for an image? To answer that question, you need to consider what the image concept is, and what direction, quality, and color of light will best illustrate it. To create a flattering portrait, using a single large softbox at a slight angle to your subject should work fine. But if you want to add some edgy highlights to a mountain bike shot to increase the tension in the image, a hard-edged light

4.23 This image was shot at 1/3200 and f/4.8 using high-speed sync and an Elinchrom Ranger. High-speed sync enables you to use f/4.8 and selective focus in sunny conditions.

source is the right choice. Your shooting distance may also influence your decision. Diffused light sources don't have much range, while a bare-bulb speedlight can shoot light far into a scene.

Let's look at how to put all this lighting technique to use. Below are two typical adventure sports shooting scenarios, and how I would go about lighting them.

Scenario #1: mountain biker

Imagine you're photographing a mountain biker on a sunny day in the mountains. The rider will pass right in front of you on a single-track trail. He is moving fast, and wearing bright colors and a helmet.

First, consider the light. Since the sun is high overhead, the light falling on the subject will come from directly overhead, resulting in some shadows under the helmet and areas on the bike. This subject needs some fill light to "snap" the colors and fill in some shadows.

One choice would be setting up a large 78-inch white Skylite reflector to bounce light back on the rider. Since you're shooting close to the subject, the reflector should bounce plenty of light into the scene. Do a test shot with the rider stationary (or an assistant standing in) on the trail and see how fast you can shoot. Use a shutter speed of 1/500 or faster to freeze the action. If it's windy outside, or if you don't have a way to anchor the Skylite, then use a speedlight instead.

The way to use a speedlight in this situation is to put it in TTL mode and make sure high-speed sync is turned on. In Nikon systems, high-speed sync is turned on in the camera custom functions; in Canon systems, high-speed sync is turned on in the flash unit. I could also use my Elinchrom Ranger at fast sync speeds using the Pocket Wizard Flex system with Hypersync. You could use your flash on camera, but for a better image, put your flash in front of the rider, aimed at his front. With the light in front of him and the sun lighting him from above, you'll get some nice cross lighting. Since you're using a speedlight close to the rider without any diffusion, high-speed sync with one flash should produce enough light. If it doesn't, add another speedlight in the same location using a Triflash bracket. Depending on the rider's speed, you should shoot at 1/500 or faster.

The final consideration is the flash-to-daylight ratio. Underexpose the daylight around 1 stop in this situation. To do so, use your camera in manual mode, set the daylight exposure to –1, and then add TTL flash triggered wirelessly using an SU800. If the distance to your flash is more than your camera can reach, use Radio Poppers as your wireless system. This would result in a fill flash lighting ratio, and the sun would still add some highlights to the top part of the rider. Don't eliminate the sun as a light source; use it as accent light in your image.

Scenario #2: half-pipe skier

In this scenario, you're hired by a ski resort to photograph a skier in the resort super pipe. They want you to capture a dramatic shot that will attract skiers to the resort. You show up and the day is partly cloudy. Your pro skier model will be at least 30 feet away from you when he does his aerial moves. He's wearing bright colors and a helmet.

As always, you begin by considering the light. If you photograph him in partly cloudy light, it will be inconsistent sun, so using a reflector is out. And aiming the reflector would be a challenge.

This means you need to use flash to add some impact to the shot. Since the skier is going to be flying through the air and you want to freeze the action, use a fast shutter speed. This means using high-speed sync flash or darkening the daylight exposure so the flash duration will freeze the action.

If I were shooting in this scenario, I would use my Elinchrom Ranger and one head with a sports reflector attached. This light setup has plenty of power to reach the skier, and will recycle fast enough so I won't miss a shot. I can choose to shoot my Ranger using Hypersync and an S-head, or underexpose the daylight 2 stops and use an A-head where the flash duration would freeze the skier. Both choices would make dramatic images in this situation.

If I'm shooting in the bottom of the pipe, I would place the light at an angle to illuminate the skier from slightly in front. Since the light will be close to me, my wireless system should have no problem

working. I might also add another light with a standard reflector on the lip of the pipe to illuminate the skier from behind. Backlighting skiers and snowboarders as they jump will add sparkle to the flying snow.

After determining my daylight exposure, I would set my main light hitting the skier to normal exposure, and the backlight to 1 stop brighter. This will result in an image with some contrast from the different intensities of the strobes. To determine my exposure, I would have an assistant stand on the lip and shoot a test shot. This would get my lights pretty close

to the right exposure, although if the skier is flying high, I might have to increase the power. I might also add a blue gel to the backlight for a more creative look.

Here's great principle to follow with your lighting: Don't illuminate the subject; *light it*. Anyone can blast light straight at a subject and illuminate it. Experiment with different angles, colors, and lighting ratios to create a masterfully lit shot, not an illuminated one. In later chapters on shooting mountain sports, winter sports, and portraits we'll look at other lighting setups.

5
Photographing Watersports

Don't worry, mon, you gonna be just fine," says a weather-beaten fisherman with a strong Jamaican accent. "Those sharks never gonna bother you."

I'm getting into my snorkel gear, watching sharks cruise around in transparent turquoise waters, and I'm not sure I believe him. At first, this sounded like a dream assignment: Go photograph a sea-kayaking trip in the Virgin Islands. Now I'm not so sure. But photographing watersports is a big part of adventure sports photography, and whatever the attendant risks—I love it.

Sea kayaking in paradise—Virgin Islands.

Water is a fluid element, and a dynamic aspect in adventure sports photography. You might photograph a kayaker paddling off a turbulent waterfall, or shoot a fisherman resting on a rock in a serene stream. Maybe you decide the best approach for a portrait is to have your subject stand waist deep in a pond. Water gives you a whole new medium to work with, and a variety of adventure sports hinge on fast-moving rivers and wavy oceans.

Keeping Your Gear Dry

Photographing watersports can mean sitting on a beach photographing sea kayakers paddling past, or it can involve shooting in the middle of a rapid with water splashing everywhere. And while most pro-level cameras and lenses can take a lot of rain, one dip into the river can spell disaster. If you want to get into watersports photography, it's time to waterproof your shooting system.

Waterproof cases and packs

In a perfect world, an adventure sports photographer can quickly bust out his camera, take a few shots, and "waterproof it" in an instant before a big wave hits. The worst thing that can happen is you don't take your camera out for a shot because you're worried about getting it wet. These moments probably make the best shots! To help you get those shots without ruining your equipment in the process, there are a number good options for keeping your gear dry and allowing quick shooting in wet environments (**FIGURE 5.1**).

One is tried and true option is a Pelican case. These hard-shell cases come in a variety of sizes and shapes, have padded interiors, and are completely waterproof. And waterproof as in you can drag your gear across a river in a Pelican case and it will be totally dry. They also float, so if your boat capsizes, your camera gear will be floating nearby.

I use a Pelican 1400 case on many of my assignments photographing watersports. This case is big enough to carry my D300s with 24–120mm f/4 lens attached, along with some flash cards and a fisheye lens for super-wide shots. When I need the camera, I just pop open the case, grab the camera, and shoot. If big waves are coming, I can put the camera back in, close the case, and be waterproof in seconds. I have threaded strong line on my case, which gives me anchor points for securing the case. When I sea kayak I will have the case mounted on my deck for easy access (**FIGURE 5.2**). On rafting and canoe trips I clip the case to the boat with a carabiner to secure it. I also use other Pelican cases, big and small, to store my camera gear on water-based trips.

Another waterproof option for quick camera access is dry bags. Rafters and sea kayakers have used dry bags for years, and their flexible, soft design makes them easy to pack in tight spots like the bow of a sea kayak. You seal these bags by folding the top flap over and clipping it down tight. If sealed properly, dry bags are watertight and will float if dropped into the water. In addition to my Pelican case on the deck of my sea kayak, I might carry a small dry bag in the cockpit with another lens or small camera. Dry bags are not rigid, so you need to be careful with your gear, but they offer another option for using camera gear in wet conditions (**FIGURE 5.3**).

Lowepro makes a waterproof backpack, the Dryzone, which keeps gear dry in wet conditions. I use the Dryzone 200. This pack can hold a lot of gear, and uses waterproof zippers and taped seams to keep things dry. I use this pack when I'm in larger boats, such as canoes and rafts.

5.1 Pelican cases loaded up ready for river travel.

5.2 Using a Pelican case allows quick access to your camera gear.

5.3 Dry bags and Pelican cases keep gear dry in wet environments.

Underwater housing

At some point, every adventure sports shooter wants to go beyond shooting all the action from the beach. I might spend hours photographing kayakers surfing in a play hole from shore. But then I wonder what the image might look like if I were in the hole with them. That's an angle you don't see every day! To accomplish that task, I will need a waterproof housing for my camera.

Underwater housings allow you to photograph at or below the surface of the water (**FIGURE 5.4**). As with waterproof cases, there are many options available. Which one you choose will depend on your shooting situation.

5.4 Using an underwater housing to shoot below the surface of the water.

5.5 Using an underwater housing to shoot at the surface.

5.6 The AquaTech speedlight housing allows triggering flashes on the surface and underwater.

The simplest and least expensive housing to use with your DSLR underwater is a flexible housing by Ewa-Marine. Ewa-Marine housings are made from clear PVC plastic, and are sealed tight by a metal bracket system at the opening. These housings come in a variety of models to accommodate almost any SLR, and offer different lens ports to match the lens used on your camera. These housings work by allowing you to push camera controls through the PVC plastic. They are waterproof from 20–150 feet, depending on the model.

The next step up is a dive housing that allows dedicated control of all your camera functions. I break dive housings into two groups: deep-dive housings and surface-sport housings. Deep-dive housings are designed with the scuba diver in mind and will operate at very deep depths. Since I'm normally photographing at the surface, or at shallow depths, I use a sport housing.

Sport housings offer some significant advantages. First, they're designed for use at the surface in rough conditions, such as breaking surf or crashing whitewater. Dive housings can purge (leak through the waterproof seal) when they get bumped, resulting in a "fish tank" effect, with your camera being the underwater coral feature. Second, sport housings offer lens ports to accommodate lenses such as the 70–200mm. Dive housings don't offer this option. Being able to use a zoom lens at the water surface opens up a lot of creative angles (**FIGURE 5.5**).

I use an AquaTech underwater housing for my Nikon D300s. This housing allows full control of all my camera features, and can take lots of rough use at the water surface. This housing is rated to stay dry to a depth of 30 feet, which is plenty deep for shooting snorkeling images. I use lens ports for my fisheye lens and 24–70mm lens, which gives me a lot of perspective choices.

AquaTech also offers another fantastic tool for my watersports photography: a waterproof housing for my speedlight (**FIGURE 5.6**). The speedlight housing attaches to the camera housing with a waterproof cable. This enables dedicated speedlight shooting, including TTL flash and high-speed sync. I can also use a Pocket Wizard Flex transmitter in the housing to trigger my Ranger system on shore. Being able to add flash to water shots like a kayaker crashing through a wave liberates my creative vision.

Fishing Images Don't Lie

Many adventure sports revolve around fast-moving, adrenaline-soaked activities. Fly fishing, on the other hand, offers the adventure sports shooter a more passive, introspective activity where the subject is directly involved with the balance of nature (catching fish). Fly fishing gives adventure sports photographers a chance to tell a story with his images—and to keep fishermen honest about what they catch.

There are many angles that work well when photographing fly fishing. Backed-off shots of fisherman enjoying the solitude of a trout stream work well, as do tight images of fly-tying. I always try to mix up my coverage of fly fishing to cover all aspects of the outing. I want to tell the story of the fishing day.

Over/under fishing images

Earlier in the book, I explained how, when composing a shot, it's important to capture fresh perspectives to keep the viewer interested. When it comes to fly fishing, here's a novel way to shift perspectives: Stop thinking about how the fisherman sees the world, and look at things from a big trout's perspective (**FIGURE 5.7**).

I like to use my underwater housing and photograph over/under shots of the fish and fisherman. To do this, I use a fisheye lens with my AquaTech housing, and shoot half the scene underwater and half the scene above water. This super-wide perspective

allows you to include more in the shot, especially important with over/under images. Try getting really close to a trout underwater with the fisherman visible above water. Be careful to keep the above-water part of the lens port dry; otherwise, you'll have big water drops in your image.

5.7 Try using an underwater housing for a unique perspective on fly fishing.

Use the fly line

Fly fishing requires casting many times to place the fly in the right spot with the right presentation. This offers great composition possibilities in the image. Better yet, fly line is often very colorful and stands out against most backgrounds. I like to use fly line as a visual handrail in my image. Sometimes I shoot broadside to the fisherman and capture the gentle arc of the line. Other times, I ask the fly fisherman to cast directly at me and have the line lead the viewer right to the fisherman in the image. For a different perspective, I shoot the backcast instead of the forward cast. This requires the fisherman to backcast directly at you while they're facing forward, but most good fisherman can do this (**FIGURE 5.8**).

Don't forget about the reel and flies themselves. I really like to attach a fisheye lens and photograph off the reel with the stream in the background. I also shoot at different shutter speeds to include motion in the image. Flies and fly cases are an important part of this activity, and make great image elements. One of my favorite fly-fishing images captures a fisherman choosing a fly in the middle of a river. With this type of shot, try shooting at a slow shutter speed to give the water a silky appearance as it flows around him to illustrate the peaceful nature of fishing, as shown in **FIGURE 5.9**.

5.9 Slow-moving water adds mood to this fly fishing shot.

5.8 Photographing a backcast in a remote stream in Alaska.

FLY-FISHING PHOTO TIPS

- Photograph above and below water for fresh views.
- Experiment with different shutter speeds to change the appearance of the moving water.
- Shoot right down the fly line to lead the viewer in the image.
- Capture images that tell a story.
- Cover all aspects of the fishing experience.

Photographing Canoeing

Canoeing is a mainstay of watersports, and can be enjoyed by anyone, anywhere. How many people first experience boating via a canoe? Canoeing presents the adventure sports shooter with a wide range of shooting options, from peaceful lake paddling in the wilderness to crashing whitewater on desert rivers.

Get close to the water

Unlike a lot of other boating adventure sports, canoeing often takes place in calm water. There is no excuse for not trying to shoot some images at the surface of the water, or even capturing some shots in the water. If you don't own an underwater housing, this is the perfect scenario for shooting at the water's edge and not worrying about getting your camera wet (**FIGURE 5.10**). Just don't fall in the lake.

I like to use a wide-angle lens, such as my 14–24mm, and photograph at the water line as the canoeist paddles past. Timing the paddle position is critical with all paddle sports. You don't want the paddle to block the subject's face, so talk with your subjects to get the timing down for your shot. I often tell canoeists to keep their paddle stroke low so their face isn't blocked as they paddle past. Try super-wide angles

5.10 Try photographing near the surface of the water in calm conditions.

5.12 Use a Manfrotto Magic Arm to photograph your own boat while you paddle.

with the paddle inches away from the lens as the canoe goes past. If you have an underwater housing, shoot some over/under images of this same scene.

Getting in the water doesn't always mean jumping in the lake. Another technique for shooting all paddle sports is shooting boat to boat. Most summers, I photograph in Alaska for a tourism bureau, and canoeing is always on their shot list (**FIGURE 5.11**). In order to capture the fun lifestyle images the client wants, I always rent two canoes. The models paddle one, and I have an assistant paddle me around in the other boat. I can photograph the other canoe against any backdrop, go in close for tight expressions, and even stand up in the boat for different perspectives.

What if you don't have a second boat, but want to create a photograph that looks like you're shooting from another boat? Break out the Manfrotto Magic

Arm (described in Chapter 6, "Photographing Mountain Sports") and attach a camera to the bow or stern. I use a fisheye lens on my camera for this shot to include as much of the scene as possible. I trigger the camera by using the self-timer, or by attaching a Pocket Wizard wireless remote firing system (**FIGURE 5.12**).

5.11 Photographing canoeing in the midnight sun of Alaska.

Rafting and Kayaking

Fly fishing and canoeing may be quiet and tranquil, but rafting and kayaking are all about heart-pumping whitewater and drama. Waiting for a kayaker to paddle off a 60-foot waterfall is a moment you won't forget. One summer I photographed kayakers paddling off Lower Mesa Falls in Idaho. I had rappelled down a cliff to get the angle I wanted. I checked and double-checked my camera and rigging system to make sure everything was right. Then I watched in awe as one kayaker after another paddled off this roaring waterfall. I'm not sure who was more pumped, the paddlers or the shooter. This is a scene every adventure sports photographer must capture!

Photographing whitewater

Photographing whitewater, whether it's rafting or kayaking, involves a lot of technique. Start by scouting the rapid and look for the best angles. Not all rapids photograph well. Some rapids may have small waves, but this means you can get really close to the action. Other rapids are so enormous that the only way to photograph them is by running them yourself (**FIGURE 5.13**). Some drops are in vertical walled gorges with minimal light and no shoreline.

5.13 Running big water in the Grand Canyon.

Safety is paramount for everyone involved in whitewater sports. If you're working with paddlers to create an image, make sure they're comfortable paddling the rapid you are photographing. Safety boaters—kayakers who are there to help if something goes wrong—are important when kayakers and rafters are paddling extreme whitewater. If I'm shooting on the shore of a big rapid, I wear a PFD (personal flotation device) in case I fall in the river.

Working with a paddler is going to net the best images. On some popular rivers you can set up by a big rapid and shoot rafters and kayakers as they come through, and get some nice images. But if you have a paddler running a rapid and coordinating with you, your images will be even better (**FIGURE 5.14**).

5.14 Working with paddlers is helpful in creating good whitewater images.

5.15 Photograph at 1/1000 or faster to freeze the action.

WHITEWATER PHOTOGRAPHY TIPS

- Scout rapids before shooting to ensure safety and good shooting angles.
- Set your camera to its fastest frame rate.
- Use predictive autofocus.
- Use a fast Compact Flash card. Consider JPEG format to get more frames before your buffer fills.
- Shoot at a shutter speed of 1/1000 or faster to freeze the action.
- Check exposure to eliminate overexposed whitewater.

Paddling whitewater is fast action defined, so set your camera frame rate to its fastest. I set my Nikon D3 to 9 fps (frames per second) to get as many frames as possible. You won't be able to script where the paddle is in the shot, so expect to see a lot of frames in which the paddler's face is blocked. Make sure you're using a fast flash card so you don't have to wait for your card to write images while you miss the action. Camera buffers typically hold more images in JPEG format than RAW. If I want to get the most frames I can before my buffer fills up, I shoot in JPEG.

I use predictive autofocus when shooting whitewater. Kayakers and rafters in rapids are moving very fast, and they'll move through your frame especially quickly if you're using a telephoto lens zoomed in on the action. Set your camera and lens to predictive autofocus to stay focused as the paddlers pass. Many lenses have a distance limitation setting where the focusing range of the lens is limited. Limiting the focusing distance speeds up the autofocus performance of the lens. If the action is taking place a significant distance from you, then apply this setting on the lens.

Shutter speed is another important consideration. If you want to freeze the spraying whitewater, start with a shutter speed of 1/1000. This should ensure sharp images. If you have enough light, shoot at even higher speeds for razor-sharp images (**FIGURE 5.15**).

Another approach is shooting whitewater really slow, around 1/4 of a second or slower. This will turn the raging rapids into a dreamy white scene. Try positioning a paddler on the shore, looking at the rapid. The silky water makes a great backdrop for a whitewater portrait (**FIGURE 5.16**).

One last point on whitewater shooting: Foaming whitewater on a sunny day can result in exposures with blown-out highlights. Check the histogram or highlight indicator on your camera LCD to make sure your exposure is correct. If the wave crests and foam are overexposed, reduce your exposure until they aren't.

Add flash to the image

A lot of whitewater photography occurs on sunny days. After all, who wants to get soaked in a river if it's cloudy and cold out? But this presents a problem to the adventure sports photographer. Helmets,

5.16 Moving water provides an interesting background for a portrait.

5.17 A Elinchrom Freelite head with sports reflector can project flash a long distance.

visors, and boulders can all add shade to the paddler, resulting in dark faces with no detail. To fix this problem, we need to add some fill flash.

The challenge of adding fill flash to whitewater images is the distance involved. If you're shooting in a raft with other paddlers, then you can use a speedlight or even a camera pop-up flash to fill in shadows under hat brims. But if you're shooting from shore, you need more power (**FIGURE 5.17**).

One solution is to use multiple speedlights on a Tri-Flash bracket aimed at where the paddler will travel. Adding more speedlights gives you more range and power, and should work for many whitewater situations. Another option is to use a larger flash system such as the Elinchrom Ranger with a sports reflector attached to the head. This system will project light very far into a scene, and can illuminate a paddler almost anywhere in a river.

In Chapter 4, "Lighting in the Field," we discussed high-speed sync. If you want to shoot faster than 1/250 using speedlights, you will need to use high-speed sync mode. This will further reduce the range of your speedlights, so you will need multiple flashes to get effective shooting distances. I often use my

Ranger and Hypersync to add flash to whitewater shots. I can easily project light 50 feet or more using one head with a sports reflector and very fast shutter speeds (**FIGURE 5.18**).

You can also freeze the action by underexposing the daylight by 2 stops or more, and rely on flash duration to freeze the subject. This technique strays from a fill flash image to a more stylized, edgy shot.

Underwater high-speed sync

Shooting with high-speed sync underwater comes with one important disclaimer. If wading into a frothing rapid with an underwater housing rigged to trigger thousands of watts of flash power precariously close to the water sounds like fun to you, then acknowledge the obvious risks and read on!

This technique came to me after exploring every option I could think of in whitewater photography. What new angle and technique was left? What new technology could change the way I shot whitewater? When high-speed sync became available for my Elinchrom Ranger, and AquaTech introduced a waterproof housing to trigger a Pocket Wizard, I knew I had my answer.

I start taking high-speed sync photography underwater by finding a safe rapid or play hole I can wade into and not get washed down river. I look for spots that have big eddies (calm, recirculating water) so if I do go for an unexpected swim, the water will be safe downstream. I work with a kayaker who can surf in the wave and be in control. I need a boater who's comfortable in this whitewater as well. I wear a full wetsuit, which keeps me warm and gives me lots of flotation if I end up swimming (**FIGURE 5.19**).

5.18 Fill flash will reduce shadows and brighten colors.

5.19 Wading into a hole to get the shot. A wetsuit will keep you warm and provide flotation.

I use my camera in an AquaTech housing with a fisheye lens attached. This means I will get a really wide-angle view, great for including the wave arching over the surfing kayaker. I attach the speedlight housing with a Pocket Wizard mini TT1 radio transmitter attached inside. This is connected to the camera housing with a waterproof cable, and will trigger my Ranger flashes onshore using Hypersync. I can shoot all the way to 1/8000 of a second using flash and my D300s (**FIGURE 5.20**).

The trick with this shot is getting into the wave action without getting your camera completely underwater. In essence, I'm trying to do an over/under image of a kayaker playing in a hole while triggering high-speed flash to add drama and freeze the action. It takes a lot of shots to capture a keeper, but when I get one, I know I have a unique shot.

5.20 Using an underwater housing and a Ranger flash in Hypersync mode made this image possible.

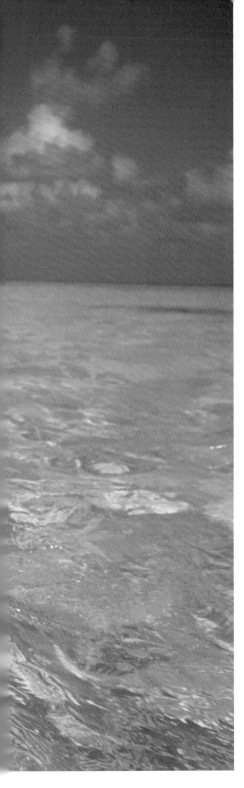

Sea Kayaking in Paradise

Sea kayaking is one of my favorite photography subjects. I spent years guiding month-long sea-kayaking trips in Patagonia, Alaska, and Baja for National Outdoor Leadership School (NOLS), and loved shooting a sunrise paddle in Baja or big crossing in Alaska. Sea kayaking offers a number of great shooting opportunities, and can be shot easily both from shore and in the water. It also offers you the chance to snorkel and get more creative underwater with your camera. Who doesn't like seeing sea kayakers idly paddling across emerald green waters in some tropical paradise?

Shooting creative angles

Start your sea-kayaking shooting working the normal angles. Try shooting boat to boat, capturing both tight shots and figures in a landscape. Paddling synchronization is also important; you don't want the paddle blocking the kayaker's face. If you're photographing a double kayak with two paddlers, make sure they stay in unison with their strokes. Out-of-sync paddlers in a double sea kayak don't look good.

I really like to use a headcam when I photograph sea kayaking (**FIGURE 5.21**). This perspective shows the viewer the paddler's point of view. I often bring my helmet with a tripod head mount on sea-kayaking trips to shoot this type of image. You can also use a lightweight headcam like the Drift HD170 or GoPro Hero for a similar angle. Another method for a POV shot using your SLR is shooting with a fisheye lens with the camera hanging from your neck. Just twist the camera strap to shorten the strap and raise the camera higher on your chest. Then hit the self-timer, grab your paddle, and start paddling until the shutter clicks. You can shoot fast and freeze the paddle, or slow and add blur to the paddle motion. Try these techniques solo or with another boater just in front of you.

Many ocean environments have steep shorelines with cliffs that provide perfect shooting locations (**FIGURE 5.22**). Climb up to shoot down on your

5.21 Using a headcam for a POV image in Prince William Sound, Alaska.

5.22 Photographing sea kayakers from a high vantage point in the Bahamas.

paddlers. Use a polarizing filter on sunny days to increase the saturation of the water and reduce glare. Look for palm trees and cactus you can photograph through with paddlers in the distance—a great technique for adding depth and a sense of place to the shot.

And since you are photographing in paradise, why not shoot in those bathtub-clear waters? Over/under images work great in sandy areas because the sand will reflect sun back up on the kayak. Shoot at midday so the sun penetrates the water, and choose

locations that are shallow with sandy bottoms. Try having someone snorkel under the kayak for this shot, or look for some interesting fish or coral to include in the underwater portion of the image.

Since the ocean is often clear, I like to snorkel down 10 feet or so and photograph sea kayakers above me (**FIGURE 5.23**). This is a really interesting angle, with the kayaker visible from below and his paddle just dipping into the water. If you're shooting on a sunny day, try positioning the sun in frame beaming through the water.

5.23 Photographing a sea kayaker from below in the Bay Isles, Honduras.

The glowing-boat shot

Are there any lighting techniques that you can use with sea kayaking? The short answer is yes, you can apply any lighting technique that I've already mentioned. You can use a simple reflector to add fill light on a sunny day, or shoot a speedlight off camera for an interesting portrait. And if you really want to get wild, you can make your sea kayak glow.

Imagine you're photographing a sea kayaker on a lake in the Tetons (not all sea kayaking takes place on the ocean) at twilight. You have the beautiful Teton range as a backdrop, and the water is flat as a pancake. As the sun sets behind the Tetons, the kayaker loses the sunlight and becomes a silhouette. This could be a nice image, so snap a few of these.

But then you decide you want some color and contrast back in the shot. Time to add a few speedlights (**FIGURE 5.24**).

To create a glowing boat and add light to the paddler in this setting, I use an Elinchrom Skyport transmitter on my camera, and attach a Skyport Universal receiver to each of the flashes. I set my flashes to manual mode with a power setting of 1/2 as a starting point. I put my flash/receiver setup in a clear ziplock bag to keep it dry, and put a flash in the bow, cockpit, and stern of the boat. I manually set the zoom range to 14mm so the flash spreads out as much as possible. The flash in the cockpit will illuminate the boat and spill onto the paddler's face. I adjust my exposure and flash output manually to get the right effect. The Skyport triggers the flashes in the kayak, making the boat glow and adding some light to the paddler. Experiment with different boat colors for different effects.

5.24 Using speedlights to create a glowing kayak.

6

Photographing Mountain Sports

Anyone who photographs adventure sports will spend a lot of time in the mountains. Mountain environments are the playground for many outdoor athletes, and the varying landscape offers much for the adventure sports photographer. Snowy peaks, massive glaciers, and towering granite walls are irresistible for the adventurer. Photography outings can range from a day trip to your local crag to month-long expeditions to distant Himalayan peaks. So grab your camera, pack up your gear, and head into the mountains.

Climbing in Eldorado Canyon, Colorado.

Camping

Any overnight trip in the mountains requires camping out. On longer expeditions, you can spend countless hours sitting in a tent waiting for the weather to improve. One summer, I spent two weeks below the west face of Mount Huntington in Alaska waiting for a break in the weather. Storm after storm dumped feet of snow on our camp, and after 2 weeks we had climbed only 3 days. Since you're likely to have downtime in camp, why not create some interesting images to document this part of your trip?

Camp life centers on your tent, and I'll be the first to admit that I choose my tents not only for their reliability in a storm, but also for their color. Luckily for the adventure sports shooter, tent manufacturers often design tents with bright colors to keep campers cheery in dismal weather (**FIGURE 6.1**). Photographing a dark green tent on the green tundra isn't going to have much impact. On the other hand, a yellow tent on green tundra will be visible from miles away.

You can take advantage of a number of interesting angles and techniques to create dramatic camping images. One of my favorite shots is using a fisheye lens and shooting from inside the tent out the door. A fisheye lens has a 180-degree angle of view and will include the tent sides, adding a nice frame to the shot. I often angle my tent toward a dramatic peak or the kitchen area of camp to provide an interesting view out the door.

CAMPING PHOTO TIPS

- Use super wide-angle lenses inside the tent to document camp life.
- Use the inside of the tent door as a frame for photographing subjects outside.
- Illuminate tents at twilight with a headlamp or speedlight to punch up color.
- Try walking through a camp scene with a headlight on to add a visual handrail in the image.

6.1 Camping on a ridge with Denali in the distance.

The other use for a fisheye lens in camp photography is photographing tent life inside the shelter. Card games, journal writing, and eating all happen inside the tent, and these activities are important images for any expedition photographer. Interior tent images give the viewer a glimpse at the camaraderie and hardship that are integral parts of camping in the mountains. Try photographing tent interiors illuminated by candlelight or flashlights. This warm glow adds a nice feel to the shot. Don't forget capturing moments in the "kitchen" as well, since camp life also centers around eating (**FIGURE 6.2**).

The other strategy of photographing camping is shooting exterior images of the tent. Brightly colored tents stand out on green and brown terrain, and add perspective to the landscape. Once I rafted down the Kongakut

6.2 Cooking the backcountry classic, macaroni and cheese.

River above the Arctic Circle in Alaska, and we used multiple yellow-dome tents for our shelters. One day we climbed a neighboring peak to look out onto the coastal plane and the Arctic Ocean. From the summit the Kongakut River valley was magnificent, and our cluster of yellow tents lent the immense valley perspective.

Tents offer another great photographic opportunity when you capture them glowing at twilight. Adding a light source in the tent will illuminate the tent and give new life to your exterior image. A number of different light sources, ranging from candlelight to speedlights, will work for this shot. Try using a gas lantern for illumination. Lanterns put out a large amount of even light and produce a cheery glow. You can adjust the lantern output based on your exposure, and work through the twilight hours into night. The advantage of using a lantern is the nice, even glow and constant light it produces. On the other hand, you probably aren't carrying a lantern on a long trip, and you have to stabilize the lantern so you don't burn a hole in your tent (**FIGURE 6.3**).

Speedlights also work well, and most photographers bring one on every backcountry outing. Place the flash on the tent floor aimed at the ceiling and set the flash zoom to wide-angle coverage. This will illuminate the entire tent, as opposed to just the top. The challenge with using speedlights is triggering the flash from outside. I use a radio trigger such as the Elinchrom Skyport to fire my flash in manual mode from outside the tent. Skyports are very small and lightweight and don't add any significant weight to the gear in your pack. To add a human element to your image, have a tentmate sit in the tent reading a book. The illumination from your light should produce a human silhouette on the tent exterior. Or have a tentmate wear a headlamp during the exposure and walk toward the camera from the tent. The headlamp will render as a bright streak, adding a visual handrail to the image.

Star trails

Want to take your camping image to the next level? Set up a shot using any of the methods above to illuminate your tent, but then keep your shutter open longer to add star trails. Star trails are a dramatic addition to any twilight or night shot, and having a glowing yellow tent in the foreground really

6.3 Glowing tents on the tundra under a midnight sunset.

adds impact to the image (**FIGURE 6.4**). To get the best results, plan on a
1-hour or longer exposure. I fasten my camera on a tripod and attach a locking cable release to the camera. I set my exposure to "Bulb" and my aperture to f/4, and focus on the glowing tent. If you're shooting a distant scene,
both the tent and stars should be in focus. My ISO will be set at 200. Long-
exposure star trails are best shot on a dark night. If the moon rises during
your exposure, the star trails will be washed out.

A very important setting to have turned on in your camera is "long exposure
noise reduction." Noise is produced during long exposures when the camera
sensor heats up, resulting in colored speckles all over the image. Over the

STAR TRAIL PHOTO TIPS

- Use wide-angle lenses, a tripod, and locking cable release for the best results.

- Use 45-minute exposures and longer to produce the best star trails.

- Turn on your camera's long-exposure noise reduction.

- Include the North Star as a central axis point for star rotation.

- To capture stars without movement, try ISO3200, 20 seconds, at f/4.

6.4 Add a glowing tent for perspective with star trail images.

course of an hour-long exposure, the noise buildup is significant, and will greatly degrade the image. But turning on your camera's noise reduction will yield a very clean final image. The camera will take the same amount of time as the initial exposure to reduce the noise. A 1-hour exposure will cause the camera to process the shot for one hour, resulting in two hours' time for one shot. Make sure you have fresh batteries in your camera before shooting a long exposure. Cameras with larger sensors will have less noise buildup than cameras with smaller sensors.

NO CABLE RELEASE

Many times I've been in the backcountry and discovered that I left my cable release at home. If I'm planning on shooting an hour-exposure star trail image, I'll have to go in a near-torpor state to hold down my shutter button for an hour. Luckily, I've found an easier way to hold the shutter open for an hour. This technique takes two items to work: a small pebble and a rubber band. Start by finding a pebble about the size of a pencil eraser and place it on top of your shutter button. Next, take your rubber band and place it around the camera body grip, coming to rest on top of the shutter button and pebble. Slowly let the rubber band push down on the pebble/shutter. If the rubber band is strong enough, it will hold down the shutter as long as you want. When the exposure is complete, carefully roll the pebble out from under the rubber band, releasing the shutter button and ending the shot. It sounds sketchy, but it works great! Hair bands and small-tent bungee cord also will work if you don't have a rubber band on hand.

Here's another way to approach glowing-tent images: Instead of shooting background star trails with a long exposure, try shooting a quick exposure to freeze the constellations in place. I shoot a Nikon D3, which has a large sensor and produces very little noise. To capture the stars without movement, I set my ISO to 3200, exposure to 20 seconds, and aperture to f/4. This will capture the stars with little movement when using a wide-angle lens. The challenging part of the exposure is getting the tent to glow without being overexposed. Try using a very small burst from your speedlight to add some glow to the shot.

Hiking

Most excursions into the mountains require hiking to get there. You can get into some remote backcountry in a four-wheel-drive vehicle, but if you're traveling in rugged terrain, the road will end at some point. Time to lace up your boots and start hiking (**FIGURE 6.5**).

Hiking in the mountains goes hand in hand with camping. On long trips, you become one with your backpack and it feels like an extension of your body. Since hiking is such a popular activity, it makes sense that active hiking images are very popular in stock photography (**FIGURE 6.6**).

Hiking photography presents a lot of creative choices. First off, how many hikers will you photograph? A single hiker can make a compelling shot, especially if you photograph one from a distance, creating a figure in the landscape. For more dynamic images, two or more hikers offer more possibilities.

6.5 Miles from nowhere: Deep in Wrangell Saint Elias National Park (right).

6.6 Hiking at sunrise in Colorado (above).

6.7 Hiking across boulders on an alpine ridge.

Photographing hikers from low angles is a great approach. I like to use my 14–24mm and photograph one hiker's boot close in the foreground leading to the second hiker on the trail. Experiment with your depth of field and decide how much of the image you want in focus. I often use an aperture of f/5.6, which will keep the foreground element in focus and background hiker just slightly out of focus. Try this same technique on foreground flowers or tree trunks with a hiker passing by in the background. Then switch your focus point so you are focused on the foreground hiker, which will put the background elements out of focus.

For a dynamic perspective, try having your hikers step or jump across rocks. Generally, you can find some big rocks and have your hiker step across them, as done in stream crossings. Position yourself below the action, and catch the hiker right as he's stepping across (**FIGURE 6.7**).

Compressing the scene

Long lenses such as the 70–200mm also work well for hiking images. With telephoto lenses, you can compress the background and narrow the angle of view. Compressing the scene is a great technique to add drama to your image. By shooting at 200mm or longer, the background appears a lot closer to the subject than it really is. This is a great way to make distant mountains and waterfalls appear to be towering over your subject (**FIGURE 6.8**).

For really dramatic effects, I use my 200–400mm with a 1.4x converter. This puts the effective focal length of my lens at 560mm, or roughly the equivalent of a pair of 10x binoculars. A few summers ago, I photographed some hikers watching a herd of caribou run past our camp. The caribou were about 100 yards away. I lined up the hikers with the passing caribou using a 300mm lens, and it looked like the hikers were almost getting trampled!

In addition to the hikers, another important compositional element in a hiking shot is the trail. Trails connect the foreground to the background in your image, and the eye will follow this visual handrail through the frame. Shoot down the trail to hikers in the distance. The viewer's eye will follow the image down the trail to the hikers.

6.8 Hiking toward distant glaciers.

Mountain Biking

Every March, when the snow starts to melt in Colorado, I start getting a little jumpy. After spending days slogging in the snow working on winter images, the idea of warm red rocks and vibrant green cottonwood trees is really appealing. That means one thing: time to go to Moab, Utah, and photograph mountain biking. Bright jerseys, colorful bikes, big air, and interesting personalities all come together in one wild adventure sport (**FIGURE 6.9**).

Big air

Mountain biking offers a number of interesting photography angles similar to hiking and trail running. Low shots, pans, blurs, and compressed figures in a landscape all work well for mountain biking. But mountain bikers like to do one activity a lot more than others: catch big air.

Mountain-bike jumps offer a dramatic, eye-catching opportunity to photograph. Two technical questions arise: What shutter speed will freeze the action? And do I need to add flash to improve the image? The easiest way to photograph mountain bikers jumping is using available light and a fast shutter speed. Ideally, you can wait for warm evening or morning light for the shot. Shooting at 1/1000 or faster should freeze the action. But another great technique is available if you're shooting in the middle of a sunny day: Photograph the mountain biker backlit by a sun star (**FIGURE 6.10**).

6.9 Miles of slickrock. Moab is mecca for mountain biking.

6.10 Sun stars create a new dynamic element in the image.

Shooting a "sun star" refers to photographing the sun with its rays shooting off in a star pattern from the sun itself. The trick is getting the exposure right to enhance the sun's rays.

The most important part of capturing an image with a sun star is using a small aperture opening of f/16 or smaller. The smaller aperture opening is what creates the rays coming off the sun. With my camera in manual mode, I start with f/16 set as my aperture, a shutter speed of 1/250, and my ISO at 200. I may have to adjust my exposure depending on what time of the day it is but, ideally, I want to underexpose my sky by about 1 stop. Darkening the sky will accentuate the sun's rays for a great starburst effect. If you pan with your subject, 1/250 may be fast enough to freeze the action. If not, then dial up your ISO to 400 or more. This will allow you to use a faster shutter speed to freeze the action. Often, I like to shoot at 1/500 or 1/1000 to freeze all movement.

If I'm shooting a sun star jump shot, or photographing a jump on a cloudy day, adding flash may improve the shot. Adding flash gives the image some pop and punches up the rider's color. Using flash also allows you to darken the sky if you want a moody, dramatic effect.

As discussed in Chapter 4, "Lighting in the Field," you can use speedlights or strobe packs in high-speed sync to add flash to an image. If you want to add fill light and keep the background pretty bright, then high-speed sync mode will allow you to shoot at 1/500 or faster to freeze the action. I like to use my Lastolite Triflash bracket with three speedlights attached to add flash to a rider. You can place this bracket on a light stand aimed at where you think the rider will fly through the air. A better solution is to have an assistant aim the speedlights at the rider as she moves through the shot so you know your flash hits the mark every time.

If you use larger strobes and don't have high-speed sync ability, then you'll be limited to your camera's flash sync speed to shoot the shot, generally around 1/250 of a second. If you are blending ambient light and studio strobe and shooting at 1/250, chances are you will get a little motion blur in the shot. This effect can be nice to include, but if you don't want any blur in the image, then you need to underexpose the ambient exposure 2 stops or more so the studio flash is the only light illuminating the subject. Since the flash is now the main light source hitting the subject, the flash duration is what will freeze the action. My Elinchrom Ranger flash pack has a flash duration of over 1/2000, plenty fast enough to freeze a mountain biker flying through the air.

You can also use larger strobe packs like the Elinchrom Ranger in high-speed sync mode using Pocket Wizards's Hypersync utility, as described in Chapter 4.

SUN STAR PHOTO TIPS

- Use an aperture opening light f/16 or smaller.
- Remove front protective filters to reduce lens flare.
- Underexpose the scene 1 stop or more to enhance the sun's rays.
- Have the sun clip a solid object in the frame to enhance its rays.

POV shot

One concept I always try to convey in my images is the excitement and adrenaline the athlete feels while riding down a slickrock trail or paddling off a waterfall. Images shot from the athlete's perspective are known as point of view, or POV, images (**FIGURE 6.11**). Let's face it: Many people will never go extreme mountain biking or kayaking. But wouldn't it be cool if they could sit on the bike while the rider blazes dow n a steep sandstone slope? Achieving that angle isn't as hard as you might think; it just takes a little do-it-yourself (DIY) rigging.

One must-have accessory for the adventure sports shooter is the Manfrotto super clamp and magic arm. This camera-mounting rig will help you capture amazing angles. The super clamp of the magic arm will attach to almost anything. Once you've attached the rig, you can articulate the arm in exactly the position you like, then tighten it down, and you're ready to go. I bought the magic arm version that has a small tripod head on one end so I can attach my camera.

For mountain biking, I like to attach the magic arm in two places. First, I attach the clamp to the rear fork of the bike tire. Next, I extend the arm out to the side with my camera attached. Finally, I run a support strap from the camera to my bike seat. This strap really helps prevent the arm from slowly lowering as you hit bumps (**FIGURE 6.12**). I use a fisheye lens to cover a full 180 degrees, and angle the lens so the ground, pedal, and handlebars are all in the frame. I like to tilt my camera on a 10-degree angle to add a little extra tension created by the diagonal line.

To trigger my camera while riding, I use a long cable release that goes from the camera along my bike frame to my handlebar grip. Or I'll use a wireless transmitter to trigger the camera while riding. If you don't have either of these, you can always set your camera to self-timer mode, dial in 10 seconds, and start pedaling down the trail. Remember to use the magic arm in the outrigger position; don't turn sharply on the side of the magic arm/camera. If you do, then your camera will start scraping across the ground.

6.11 The rider's view of the White Rim Trail in Canyonlands National Park.

MOUNTAIN BIKING PHOTO TIPS

- Use ground-level, wide-angle perspectives to create dynamic scenes.

- Try a shutter speed of 1/30 as a starting point for pan-and-blur images.

- Use a shutter speed of 1/1000 or faster to freeze the action.

- Use special accessories like the Manfrotto super clamp or a head cam to get unique "rider's perspective"/POV shots.

6.12 A Manfrotto magic arm and super clamp allow remote positioning of your camera, as shown in the image on the left, and enable you to get shots like the one seen on the right.

A less precarious place to position the magic arm is the front handlebars. With the clamp attached here, you can position the arm and camera off to one side looking back at the rider on the bike. Just be careful the magic arm stays out of the frame. The front handlebar position is great for photographing multiple riders behind the front rider. You can carefully position the other riders in a nice, graphic line leading back from the front rider.

There are other methods of creating POV images that don't require a magic arm but do require a helmet. Affectionately known as the helmet-cam angle, this shot looks right down the arms of the rider from atop his head. If you use a fisheye lens, you can see most of the rider's arms and all of the handlebars.

Helmet cams come in a variety of sizes, resolution, and quality. Since I'm a Nikon shooter, I've devised a way to get helmet cam shots using my existing camera gear. I drilled a hole into an old climbing helmet and mounted a tripod head on the outside using a standard 3/8-inch screw through the helmet. I use my D300s and a fisheye lens as my camera setup. I use a Pocket Wizard wireless remote to trigger my camera. To duplicate this setup, you'll need an accessory motor drive cable from Pocket Wizard to trigger the camera. This system works great, and remote camera triggering can be used in other adventure sports photography scenarios.

SPECIALTY HEAD CAMS

The only downside to having a full-size DSLR on your head when you're riding is its weight. Bounce down the trail with a DSLR on your head and you'll find yourself eating some ibuprofen to dull your headache at the end of the day. A less cumbersome option is a specialty head cam such as the Drift HD170 Stealth or GoPro Hero (**FIGURE 6.13**). These lightweight cameras can be attached to almost anything, from surfboards (in a waterproof housing) to helmets. They take 5-megapixel still images at varying time intervals, from 2 seconds to 1 minute to more than 2 hours. And both of these head cams also shoot 1080p HD video.

6.13 A lightweight head cam like the GoPro captures images and video of the athlete's view.

Rock Climbing

Before I was a photographer, I was a climber. My climbing obsession started on the sandstone spires of Garden of the Gods in Colorado. My brother tied me to the end of a rope and said, "You lead." I was hooked. Climbing became my sole focus for many years after college. I lived in the back of my truck and traveled across the country, climbing, guiding clients, and having memorable adventures. I always had my camera in hand, documenting remote expeditions into the mountains. Later, my passion changed from wanting to climb myself to capturing the activity on film. I realized I needed to share my passion for climbing and the environment with others (**FIGURE 6.14**).

Photographing rock climbing takes things up a notch, both in the technical aspect and the risk. Fifth-class climbing, where climbers use ropes and place protection to lead a route, is a serious endeavor. As a photographer, your safety and that of the other climbers can rest entirely on your shoulders. Imagine dropping a lens or even a small flash card. If you're shooting from above at climbers below you, one small item dropped becomes a missile that can distract or even knock a climber off the route (**FIGURE 6.15**). Be careful!

Can you still create decent rock-climbing images if you're not a climber? Absolutely! As with any sport, the more you know about it, the more you'll be able to anticipate the action. But photographing rock climbing doesn't always mean hanging off ropes above the climber.

One low-risk climbing activity that photographs well is bouldering. Bouldering involves climbing on boulders and rocks close to the ground with no ropes or belayers. This means you can photograph from the ground level, or scramble on top of an easy rock to shoot down (**FIGURE 6.16**). Since you're photographing on the ground, bouldering offers easy options to use flash. Just put up your strobes on light stands as you would on a normal photo shoot.

6.14 Climbing Steve's Arete on Mount Lemmon near Tucson, Arizona (right).

6.15 Shooting from above climbers generally offers the best perspective (above).

6.16 Photographing bouldering allows you to create great images without using ropes.

6.17 Always search out new angles for photographing climbers.

360-degree shooting

Bouldering also allows you to get really close to your subject. My approach to photographing bouldering is the "360-degree method." When I teach photo workshops, I often ask the participants how many of their photos they take while standing up, holding the camera at eye level? Perhaps 70 percent, 80 percent, maybe even 90 percent? Boring! The whole world can grab a camera, point, and shoot. This is your moment to show the world your creativity. Get down in the dirt, climb up on the rock, or put the camera right on the climber's hand. Let your creativity shine!

The 360-degree method is my way of reminding me that I need to cover every angle of the activity. It's very easy, as a photographer, to become complacent and stand in the same spot for an entire shoot. Since bouldering is done close to the ground, it lets me maneuver all around my subject. I experiment with shallow depth of field, focusing on the climber's hand for one shot, and in the next shot focusing on the hold they're trying to grab. I lie on the ground below the climber and grab a wide-angle shot at their foot on a small hold.

I also like to capture climber's chalk as the climber's hand hits a hold. To do this, focus on the hold, then have the climber chalk up and slap the hold. You should end up with a puff of white powder in your shot. The climber is near the ground, so explore all the angles. And if a roped team is just starting a climb, then photograph them from all angles as well (**FIGURE 6.17**).

Bounce flash

When most photographers think about bounce flash, they think of a white ceiling in a small room. But photographing bouldering offers a great chance to use bounce flash. Adding a little bounced light can turn silhouettes into colorful images, or just add a little catch light into the climbers' eyes.

Here is the technique I use to bounce flash for bouldering images, and all it takes is a reflector, speedlight, and TTL flash cord. Start by attaching the dedicated TTL flash cable to the camera hot shoe and flash. I use a Nikon SC28 cord, which gives me 9 feet of cable to use, more than enough for most of my shots. If I need more room, I can tether a second SC28 cable to the first one, giving me 18 feet of distance between camera and flash.

6.18 Bounced fill flash adds color to an image without overpowering the shot.

Next, open up your collapsible reflector. I like to use a Lastolite TriGrip reflector. These reflectors have a handle and allow easy, one-hand maneuvering. If I want to add a warm glow to the shot, I use soft gold as the reflector surface. If a neutral tone is better, then I choose white. I aim the flash at the reflector, bouncing the light back onto the climber. Since the reflector is a large surface, the light reflected on the climber is very soft (**FIGURE 6.18**).

It's easier to have an assistant or another climber hold the reflector and flash so you can concentrate on your angle. The real question, when using this technique, is what flash-to-ambient-light ratio to choose. Since the flash is attached to a dedicated TTL cable, the camera will still evaluate output in TTL mode. I shoot in a balanced fill flash mode, which generally puts me pretty close to the right exposure for both flash and ambient light right at the start. If I want an almost imperceptible flash for just a touch of highlights, I lower the speedlight output around 1–2 stops to get just the right blend of flash and ambient light.

On a rope

Most climbing photographers know that butt shots are not a good idea. Sometimes, shooting climbers from below works fine, especially if you're far enough away from the cliff. But shooting with a telephoto lens right up at a rock climber from below gives you not only a butt shot, but a tight butt shot—not good. Time to grab your climbing gear and get on a rope above the climber.

LEARN THE ROPES

Ascending lines and working with camera gear should be done only by experienced climbing photographers. If you don't know anything about using ropes and setting up anchors, take a rock-climbing course to learn these skills. Hands-on learning is critical to mastering these skills. Programs like NOLS offer 2-week climbing courses that give you a solid foundation of climbing skills. Once you've mastered the basics, practice ascending lines and getting your systems down solid before you work with climbers. You have to have your ascension and rope technique wired or you'll be overwhelmed with dealing with rope systems instead of focusing on your shot.

FIGURE 6.19 Adding fill flash will improve color in your image, as in this shot, taken climbing on the Poudre Canyon wall in Colorado.

Photographing climbers from above gives you a front-row seat to the tension climbers exhibit while rock climbing. Gripping expressions and long reaches will give the viewer sweaty palms. When I shoot while anchored to a rope above climbers, I streamline everything I need to do with my cameras. Dropping anything on climbers below is unacceptable. I often carry two camera bodies with me, one with a 17–35mm lens attached, the other with a 70–200mm. This allows both close-up, wide-angle images and telephoto shots from farther away. Photographing down a crack at a climber is a great telephoto image. Another lightweight option would be using one camera body with a 24–120mm or 28–135mm lens. Make sure your camera straps arc secured and the cameras are around your neck or clipped into your body using locking carabiners. I use high-capacity SanDisk 16 and 32 MB flash cards to eliminate having to switch cards during a shoot. If you're on a big wall climb for multiple days, then try to do any lens or flash card switching at a belay ledge. This way, if you do drop something, it probably won't go far.

TTL flash can also be used while photographing from a rope. Generally, the best option is for the flash to be on camera and used in fill flash mode. This will add a pop of light to the climber and blend well with the surrounding rock. If you're shooting on an overcast day, then fill flash really helps. Just be careful not to bang your flash and snap it right off. If you need more light, then it's time to bring out the big guns (**FIGURE 6.19**).

The big guns

I'll admit it: I'm addicted to big strobes. My friend and lighting guru, Mark Astmann at Manfrotto, calls me a *flashaholic*. Adding your own light to a scene gives you a whole new set of creative options. But how can you add big strobes to a rock-climbing image? If you're high on a route, then you're better off using speedlights. But if you're on a one-pitch climb (a "pitch" refers to a rope length, or around 165 feet), then you have big light options.

First, you need a battery-powered strobe system to use at the crag. I use my Elinchrom Rangers and Quadras (as described in Chapter 4), which give me plenty of power to light a shot. Since the Rangers are 1100 watts and heavier, I use these on the ground to shoot light at climbers on a route. I use sports reflectors on the flash head to project the light even

farther. Often, using just one light will add lot of drama to a shot.

My favorite time to shoot big strobes is at twilight. The sky is usually deep blue and purple, and the beam of flash hitting a climber is very striking. I use the Elinchrom Skyport system to trigger the flashes from a distance. The beauty of Skyports is that not only do they trigger flashes a long way away, but you can also control flash output right at the camera by using the Skyport output buttons.

Although the Rangers have more power, the Quadras are smaller and lighter, and thus offer more portability. The Quadras have really liberated my rock-climbing flash photography (**FIGURE 6.20**). I can carry them farther into the backcountry, and place them in precarious positions. Using tall light stands, I use the Quadras for a cross-lighting shot.

6.20 Lightweight flash packs such as the Elinchrom Quadra offer exciting new possibilities for photographing rock climbing.

The Quadra cross light

One challenging aspect of lighting rock climbers is getting the lights into position to create an edgy shot. You can do only so much with lights when you're shooting up from the ground at a climber. The next step is getting the lights right near the climber so you can really create some dramatic lighting, and one of my favorite techniques is cross lighting.

Cross lighting involves positioning two lights across from one another with your subject in the middle. My main light is generally a small softbox, and my kicker (accent) light is a flash head that's shot through a sports reflector. This cross-lighting setup gives you very dramatic lighting, and you can underexpose the daylight for even more effect.

To position the lights near the climber, I use Manfrotto 269HDBU super-high stands. These stands are very durable and extend to 24 feet, which is plenty of distance off the ground to capture a climber on a route. I use climber's webbing and a locking carabiner to attach the pack to the metal bracket at the top of the stand. These stands have a leveling leg that moves independently of the other legs, which is very handy for working on uneven terrain.

Finally, I add sandbags to the base and send up the lights on either side of the climber. I've used this setup in a slight breeze, and the stands are rock solid. Since the Quadras have built-in Skyport receivers, I can trigger and control output from the Skyport transmitter on my camera.

Once the lights are set up, I ascend a rope to get above the climber for the shot. If possible, I have the climber repeat the section that the lights are set up to illuminate. This cross-lighting approach takes coordination with your climbers—unlike the typical available light-shooting method, where the climbers move at their own pace. But the results are worth the effort (**FIGURE 6.21**).

FIGURE 6.21 Cross lighting a rock climber produces a fresh look.

7

Photographing Winter Sports

Winter is one of the best times for adventure sports photography. The snowy mountains are bathed in deep powder, and long ribbons of blue ice hang from the cliffs. Ski areas are open, and snowboarders grab big air in the super pipes. The shooting is more difficult in the cold and snow, but the rewards are worth it.

Nature serves up one of its most spectacular displays in winter, providing a great subject for the adventure sports photographer: the Northern Lights.

Navigating ice fins and blue glacier pools in Alaska.

Shooting the Northern Lights

The Northern Lights, or Aurora Borealis, appear when charged particles from solar winds hit our atmosphere. These charged particles hit oxygen and nitrogen at different elevations in our atmosphere, creating the different colors of the display (**FIGURE 7.1**). Green is the color you'll see most often, but dramatic displays of red and purple can also occur.

I'll never forget the first time I saw the Northern Lights. I was guiding a group on a 300-mile Arctic river trip in Alaska. We had been hiking and paddling for 5 weeks, and had arrived at Noatak, a small bush community situated on the river. Normally, when camping in Alaska, you stay in a tent to avoid mosquitos and the rain. But this night we decided to sleep outside since it was a clear night and the cold August temperature had eliminated most of the mosquitos. By late August, Alaska has darkness at night, unlike earlier in the summer when the sky stays lit at night. The sun barely dips below the horizon this far north in the summer, and some Arctic communities get 24 hours of daylight.

I awoke in the middle of the night and casually looked up at the night sky. I couldn't believe my eyes. The sky was on fire with dancing red, green, and purple light beams shooting across the sky. It seemed impossible for such a light display to be occurring naturally. But the light show continued, and unlike many Northern Lights displays, this kaleidoscope of colors continued for hours.

NORTHERN LIGHTS PHOTO TIPS

- Always use tripods and locking cable releases.
- Turn on your camera's long exposure noise reduction.
- Start with an exposure of 30 seconds, f/2.8 at ISO400. Proper exposure depends on the intensity of the Northern Lights at the time and place you see them.
- Experiment with car lights streaking past or glowing tents in the foreground for different perspectives.
- Bring extra batteries to switch out cold ones.

Photographing the Northern Lights is similar to shooting images of stars. You'll need a tripod, cable release, and fresh battery. Depending on how bright the display is, start with an exposure of 30 seconds at ISO400 at f/2.8. Check your histogram and adjust your exposure accordingly.

7.1 The Northern Lights are frequently seen during the winter in Alaska.

Ice Climbing

Photographing ice climbing is similar to shooting rock climbing, but with three major differences. First, your fingers are going to be numb. Second, the climbing medium can be very fragile and crash down on people below. And third, there are a lot of sharp and pointy objects that like to penetrate Gortex and skin. Sound fun? You bet (**FIGURE 7.2**)!

Winter environments have a mood of their own. Photographing a brightly clad climber as he inches up a blue ribbon of ice is a beautiful photographic moment for the adventure sports shooter (**FIGURE 7.3**). Cold can hinder camera and photographer performance. Make sure you're dressed (see (Chapter 1, "Pack the Right Gear") for the elements.

7.2 Photographing ice climbing can be cold and harsh, but the results are worth it (opposite).
7.3 An ice climber leading Bridal Veil Falls in Valdez, Alaska (below).

7.4 Crampons and ice tools are great subject matter for ice-climbing images.

7.5 Ice formations change every year, offering new angles on the same route.

I always carry spare batteries for my camera in the winter. I keep one in my pocket, where my body heat keeps it warm. If my battery starts to fail due to the cold, I switch out batteries. Generally, at temperatures above zero, most modern DSLR cameras and batteries do well. If it gets well below zero, then your battery life will decrease.

One important item to remember is to avoid being directly under an ice climber as she hammers away at a route. Falling ice is a normal part of this activity, and you don't want to be in the firing zone. The same applies if you are photographing ice climbers from above. You need to be very careful not to knock off ice that can hit a climber below.

Since ice climbers use ice tools and crampons to ascend, this gives you a new element to focus on in your images. Try shooting just off the crampon (staying to the side of the climber) to highlight the sharp points of the crampon (**FIGURE 7.4**). Experiment with different shutter speeds to capture the climber as he hammers away at the ice. Try adding a little flash to capture the flying ice. Just remember: If you're wearing crampons, don't step on any ropes.

Ice formations can also add a unique aspect to ice-climbing images. Some routes will have huge curtains of ice, providing a giant translucent blue wall for a climber to ascend (**FIGURE 7.5**). The climber will be a silhouette on a wall of glowing blue ice. Other times, giant narrow pinnacles of ice freeze down cliff faces, providing stunning compositions. Every winter brings a new variety of ice-climbing formations for climbers to tackle; you just have to get out and photograph them!

Mountaineering

Mountaineering is the quintessential mountain sport (**FIGURE 7.6**). Long before camping and rock climbing became popular recreational activities, epic mountaineering expeditions were occurring in remote mountain ranges around the world. Gripping sagas like Maurice Herzog's *Annapurna* planted the seed for my interest in mountaineering. And from the first day I took up

the sport, no matter how heavy my pack, I've always carried my camera.

Photographing mountaineering presents its own set of challenges. Most mountaineering trips are multi-day excursions, and can even be many weeks long. Packing the right gear and means to power your cameras is a big concern (see Chapter 1). The weather can be the most severe of any adventure sports activity. I've spent days stuck in snow caves in Alaska enduring 80-mile-an-hour winds and bitter temperatures. Not only do you have to prepare yourself to deal with these conditions; you have to make sure your camera gear is ready as well. And photographing mountaineering often means you're on a rope team to protect yourself against crevasse falls (**FIGURE 7.7**). You have to coordinate with your rope team to get the right angle for your images.

The appeal of photographing mountaineering is the raw beauty that surrounds this sport. You're living in the mountains in a tent, watching the light unfold around you. You live, breathe, and sweat just like your fellow climbers, allowing you to capture intimate details that may range from a successful summit bid to digging out your tent in a numbing storm.

I like to incorporate a lot of the landscape in my mountaineering images. Successful mountaineering trips hinge on environmental factors such as weather, terrain, and conditions. Documenting a rope team traveling through an icefall, or climbers

7.6 A climber at 22,000 feet stares at the summit of Nanda Devi, India.

7.7 Photographing from a rope team is often necessary on mountaineering trips.

7.8 Subzero camping high on Denali.

approaching a summit makes a compelling image. On the same note, photographing tents getting hammered by a storm or ice caves in subzero temperatures will also yield dramatic shots (**FIGURE 7.8**).

One of my most memorable experiences photographing adventure sports occurred while shooting a mountaineering trip in India. I was camped on an icy ridge around 19,000 feet on Nanda Devi, a 25,000-feet-high Himalayan peak. I was part of an Indo-American climbing team attempting the east peak. I decided to venture out one night to photograph our tents in the moonlight with Nanda Devi in the distance. As I was setting up my tripod, I kept hearing noises behind me. Since my climbing partners were asleep, I figured it was the wind—until I heard heavy, raspy breathing right behind me.

Looking over my shoulder, I saw something big moving my way in the moonlight. I blinked in disbelief, and became a firm believer in the abominable snowman at that moment. Without getting a shot, I scurried back across the ridge and jumped into my tent. The next morning I went back to the site of my encounter, and found snow leopard tracks all over the ridge. It isn't every day you run into a snow leopard in the middle of the night on an icy ridge at 19,000 feet.

The key to success shooting mountaineering images is having your camera ready, which I didn't that night (I was scrambling for my tent). This means around your neck, ready to shoot quickly. If you're part of a rope team, the last thing you want to do is to make them stop while you dig your camera out of your pack (**FIGURE 7.9**).

7.9 Climbers on a rope team traversing a crevassed area.

Depending on the terrain, I often shoot while walking. I like to use a camera with a lighter body like the Nikon D300s and one zoom lens for my shooting. I put my camera in a very compact case like the Lowepro Toploader Zoom 55, which also has a waterproof cover. This case also offers other harness systems if you don't want to carry it around your neck. I find that carrying mine around my shoulder works well and is comfortable . In camp, I'll break out more lenses and take more time to set up images. But when I'm traveling during the day, I go with one body and lens, and ensuring that they're lightweight is key to avoid a sore neck.

WILD ANGLES FOR WILD PLACES

Remember headcam shooting in mountain biking? You can do the same thing in mountaineering and really show the viewer what you're experiencing. I like to shoot headcam angles when I'm on the edge of a big crevasse or climbing a ridge. Use a fisheye lens to show as much as possible. To keep things simple, just set your self-timer and hit the shutter button.

A variation on this approach is to let the camera dangle on the neck strap and shoot images from chest level instead of on your head. Try shooting down the rope to other rope team members in front on you. The rope provides a colorful curving line to guide the viewer through the shot. Or try shooting a climber's crampon at ground level in the foreground and other climbers in the distance. If you really want to create a extreme image, try including crevasses in the shot.

Take the plunge

One environmental feature mountaineering images offer that aren't found in other types of adventure sports shooting is crevasses. Crevasses are cracks in the glacial ice ranging from small seams you can step over to huge cracks big enough to swallow tents. True, as a mountaineer, you try to avoid these nasty gaping holes. But for photographers, crevasses provide a fresh perspective. Crevasses are dangerous places to shoot, and you need to know crevasse rescue systems inside and out before setting up a shoot near them. When in doubt, always be conservative with what you photograph. As the saying goes, "There are old mountaineers, and bold mountaineers, but there are no old, bold mountaineers." Replace the word "mountaineers" with "photographers" and you'll get the idea.

Once I had an assignment photographing mountaineering rangers on Denali (also known as Mount McKinley) for *Alaska* magazine. These rangers do high-altitude patrols during the climbing season on Denali, and frequently are called on for rescues. A critical part of their training is learning how to extricate themselves and other climbers from crevasses. In other words, I landed an assignment to go jump in crevasses with my camera and shoot photos (**FIGURE 7.10**). One of the coolest angles I discovered was shooting from inside a crevasse while a climber stepped across it above me.

Unlike a journalistic approach, where you're documenting daily activities of an expedition as they occur, shooting crevasse images will take some coordination with other climbers. You don't just happen

MOUNTAINEERING/ ICE-CLIMBING PHOTO TIPS

- Bring extra batteries to switch out cold ones.
- Seek out interesting ice formations and curtains for unique images.
- Try using the rope as a leading line in your composition.
- Experiment with slow shutter speeds to capture swinging ice tools and flying ice.
- Don't attempt shots that are beyond your level of mountaineering experience, and be cautious; mountaineering and ice-climbing photography present very high objective hazards.

7.10 Mountaineering rangers practicing crevasse rescue on the Kahiltna Glacier.

7.11 Shooting from inside a crevasse is challenging, but produces dramatic results.

to be in a crevasse when a random climber steps over. The critical part of shooting from inside a crevasse is finding a crevasse location that is safe and not too big. On many glaciers, you can find mellow crevasse fields that aren't very active and are relatively safe. You can even walk right out the end of some snow-filled crevasses. You do not want to shoot in deep, vertical crevasses! Look for cracks that aren't deep and have a solid hard lip without a lot of soft snow. You need to find a crack with solid edges a climber can easily step across. On big glaciers, I often find snow-filled crevasses that work perfectly for these types of images. Make sure the crevasse isn't too big—no falling allowed (**FIGURE 7.11**).

If creating this shot sounds difficult, it is. I work only with very experienced mountaineers with whom I feel completely comfortable when creating this type of image. They need to be belayed and have safe landings if they're jumping over a crack. But the resulting shot is incredible, and bound to catch a viewer's attention.

Skiing and Snowboarding

What could be better than gliding through fresh powder on a sunny day in the mountains? Capturing it on film! Downhill skiing, cross-country skiing, and snowboarding are very popular, and make great subjects for the adventure sports photographer. Resort skiing and snowboarding allow you maximum shooting time on the slopes and access to some scenic terrain (**FIGURE 7.12**). Cross-country and backcountry skiing have no limits and lots of untracked powder. Skiing in the backcountry also means no groomed slopes, so you need to be aware of avalanche danger and pack avalanche rescue gear such as transceivers, shovels, and probes. Another option is heli-skiing, which offers the most dramatic mountain backdrops and endless tracked powder but, at a price tag of about $900 a day, it isn't cheap.

7.12 Ski resorts offer concentrated shooting in terrain parks.

Every winter I buy a pass to one of the ski areas in Colorado. I really enjoy shooting at Copper Mountain. It has a great terrain park, huge super pipe, lots of scenic backgrounds, and great skiing. Better yet, it doesn't seem as crowded as other Colorado ski areas. I can get enough runs in that, by the end of the day, my legs are Jell-O. The trick when shooting at a resort is how to carry gear on the lift, and that's where the right pack really helps.

I use a Lowepro Flipside 400 AW as my skiing pack. This pack is large enough to hold multiple speedlights, and a lens and camera, yet still has a slim profile. When I get on the lift, I just take off one shoulder strap and rotate the pack to my front side for easy carrying. But what I really like about this pack is that it opens from the shoulder-strap side. If I'm in deep powder and don't want to put my pack on the ground, I simply rotate it around to my front side, unzip the main compartment, and get whatever gear I need. I never have to put my pack on the ground.

Powder pockets

One key ingredient to many great skiing and snowboarding photos is fresh powder. Snow flying through the air adds a dynamic element to the shot. Powder shots create "I wanna be there" photos. What skier or rider doesn't want to make first tracks in powder? Obviously, you need fresh powder to create this type of image, but how often do freshly fallen snow and your availability to shoot match up? Don't worry; there's fresh powder almost every day at most ski areas; you just have to find it (**FIGURE 7.13**).

When I ski at Copper Mountain, I know that certain runs feature "snow eddies" that, 90 percent of the time, have untracked powder. An eddy is a river feature where water recycles upstream behind a boulder or large object in the river, creating sort of a deposition zone. "Snow eddy" is a term I coined for pockets of snow adjacent to a ski run that skiers don't ski because they're off the main run (but still in bounds). These pockets can have fresh powder days after the last storm.

I will set up my shot in these powder pockets, prefocus where the skiers or riders will come through, and fire away as they make fresh tracks and blast

7.13 Look for untracked terrain and powder between groomed runs at ski resorts.

7.14 Snowboarding through untracked areas at Copper Mountain, Colorado.

powder everywhere. If it's a sunny blue day, conditions can't get much better. Oftentimes I can shoot multiple runs through the same powder pocket (**FIGURE 7.14**).

Skiing is a fast-moving activity. If I want to use any fill flash, I need high-speed sync to freeze the action (see Chapter 4, "Lighting in the Field"). Both the Lastolite TriFlash and Quad Bracket rig work well to provide enough flash power and stop the action, and these brackets fit easily in my Lowepro pack. I use my Radio Poppers or Pocket Wizard system with the speedlights to enable high-speed sync and avoid signal interference from the sun. Using radio transmitters also allows me to get farther away from my lights for different angles. To plant my speedlights in the snow, I attach the TriFlash bracket to the pointed end of my ski pole. My ski poles have removable baskets, so I can take the basket off and attach the bracket to this end. I plant the handle end in the snow or have an assistant hold the ski pole.

Pipe shots

With the popularity of snowboarding exploding at resorts, ski areas have designed elaborate terrain parks and half pipes for riders. Both skiers and snowboarders will ride these features, offering the photographer a whole new winter venue to photograph. Jumps are the norm here, so get ready for fast action and precision timing with your shots.

Super pipes are one of my favorite areas to photograph skiers and snowboarders (**FIGURE 7.15**). I grew up skateboarding pools and half pipes, so I was naturally attracted to half-pipe riding at ski areas. Photographing half-pipe jumps can be fairly straightforward. I use a fast shutter speed of 1/1000 or faster, set my motor drive to 9 frames a second on my Nikon D3, and prefocus on where the rider will be. Often, you can't see the rider until he pops off the lip, so having your focus set will facilitate getting the maximum number of images. If I can see the rider the entire time, or if I'm shooting him at a number of different points in the pipe, I set my autofocus to continuous servo and set the focus pattern to a 9-point group. These settings enable the camera to keep sharp focus on the rider as long as I get my focus point near my subject.

Using big strobes is a great technique for photographing half-pipe riding. I like moody, dramatic half-pipe shots, so I set my ambient (daylight) exposure 2–3 stops underexposed and rely on flash duration to freeze the subject. Underexposing the daylight ensures that the flash is what illuminates my subject, and therefore flash duration is what

7.15 A snowboarder grabbing the lip at Copper Mountain, Colorado.

7.16 Flash duration, not shutter speed, freezes the action when you underexpose the ambient light.

freezes the action. My Elinchrom Rangers have a very fast flash duration and can easily stop the action. Even though my shutter speed will be 1/200 of a second, the fast flash duration will freeze the action (**FIGURE 7.16**).

I set up my main light back off the lip of the pipe, aimed at the point where the rider will be flying in the air. I determine flash exposure by having an assistant stand right near the lip, fire a test shot, and check my LCD histogram for exposure data. This is approximately the distance the rider will be during his jump, only higher up. I adjust the flash power until my histogram shows the right exposure. After the first jump, I double-check my exposure and change the output if needed.

In addition to one-light setups, I also like to shoot two-light setups for snowboarding photography. I start by setting up my main light as described above. Then I set up a second light in the bottom of the pipe, aimed at where the rider will fly off the lip. I set the power of this flash to be about 1 stop brighter than the main light to add an edgy highlight. When snowboarders or skiers launch off the lip, they often kick up snow as they get airborne. Adding a second light from below aimed at this spot will give a dramatic backlight effect to the flying snow, and add more dimension to the shot. If you shoot at twilight, this two-light set up works really well.

Seaming up the shot

A great technique in post-production is combining a number of jumping images into the same shot. These images could be a skier jumping off a cliff, or a snowboarder getting big air at a terrain park. First, you need to be shooting on a tripod to capture any images you hope to combine later on. All the shots must line up perfectly in the final composite, or the sequence image won't work. Second, set your motor drive to as fast as it will go. I shoot at 9 frames per second to capture every part of a big jump. Next, set your exposure and focus to be consistent for every frame. You want to have identical images for every frame so that when they're combined, everything meshes perfectly. The only thing that changes is the skier's position as he moves through the air frame by frame (**FIGURE 7.17**).

7.17 Sequence images are easy to produce in Photoshop.

Combining the images in the computer is easy. Start by opening the first image in the sequence in Photoshop (**FIGURE 7.18**).

Next, open the second shot. Choose the Move tool and, while pressing the Shift key, move this image on top of the first image (**FIGURE 7.19**).

Holding the Shift key down while doing this move ensures perfect alignment with the underlying image. Close the image you just added to the top of the first layer. Now add a mask to the second image layer and fill it with black (**FIGURE 7.20**).

SINGLE-FRAME ACTION SEQUENCE PHOTO TIPS

- Set your camera to manual exposure and focus. You need consistent frames to create the sequence.

- Use the fastest motor drive mode you have for maximum number of frames.

- Use a fast flash card to avoid having card writing stop the frame sequence.

- Use a tripod to keep the frame identical for each shot.

7.18 The first image in the sequence.

7.19 Move the second image on top of the first image.

This will hide everything in the layer. Choose the Brush tool, make sure your foreground color is set to white, and brush over where the skier should be in the image. The top-layer skier magically appears, but in a slightly different position than the skier in the first image (**FIGURE 7.21**).

Repeat the above steps for the remaining images in your sequence, each time revealing the skier in a new position (**FIGURE 7.22**).

When you have applied this technique to all the frames, you should have an image of a skier captured multiple times in the same frame.

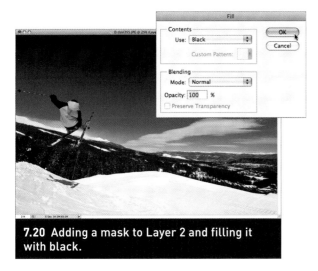

7.20 Adding a mask to Layer 2 and filling it with black.

7.21 Brush (with white as foreground color) the black layer mask to reveal the top-layer skier shown here.

7.22 Repeat the steps above with all the sequence frames to create the composite.

8

Portraits

When I first started photographing adventure sports, all I wanted to do was capture the wild activities taking place around me. Who would believe a climber could pull up on that hold? Was a kayaker really paddling off that waterfall? My adventure photography focused on the boldness and wildness of the activities. But who were the athletes doing these extreme sports?

As my career developed, I began to realize I was missing a big part of the picture in my photography. I had lots of activity shots, but no close, personal portraits of the people doing these activities. These were the same kind of people I had guided with for years. They lived and breathed their passion for the outdoors. Yet these wilderness professionals were not in my sights as a photographer.

A large softbox creates dramatic light against a stormy sky in this portrait, taken at the crags in Colorado.

I began to shift my focus to portrait photography. I needed to put a face on the athletes I was photographing. How could I connect the viewer with the athlete in an image? What techniques and lighting would accomplish this task? The more I shot portraits, the more I identified the key components for a successful shot.

Ultimately, I developed this formula for creating portraits: *Great portraits are a combination of relevant location, good rapport, effective use of light, and impeccable technique.*

Location, Location, Location

Once you have a subject to photograph, the next decision you need to make is where to photograph them. Location can make or break a portrait. Locations can be of primary importance, or can be secondary in importance to the subject. Is the background telling more about the subject, or just a distraction? Which backgrounds really contribute to the effectiveness of a portrait?

The good news for adventure sports portraits is there are many ripe locations just begging to be used in the shot. Your studio is the outdoors, and it offers endless options. Don't let beautiful locations go to waste; use these scenes to make a stronger shot.

Environmental portraits

Environmental portraits use location as an important element in the shot. The background provides information about the subject being photographed, and contributes a lot to the shot. In some cases, the environment may be as important to the image as the subject.

Creating environmental portraits is my favorite approach to photographing adventure sports athletes. I begin by considering my subject, and what activity they do, and identifying the obvious choice for a background (**FIGURE 8.1**). Kayakers look great photographed with rivers behind them. The same

works with fishermen. A climber can look good at the crags, leaning against a boulder, or even roping up in an indoor climbing gym. Mountain bikers work well with backgrounds of desert and mountains behind them; this is the terrain they ride.

Don't limit yourself to the obvious backgrounds for your portrait. When shooting sea kayakers, for example, think about what they really do. They paddle mile after mile on oceans and lakes, spending hours, days, and weeks on the water. The obvious backdrop for sea kayakers is the ocean or lake. But how about mixing it up and putting them in the water? Try putting them neck deep in the water holding their paddle. Do the unexpected and get creative (**FIGURE 8.2**). Draw the viewer into your portrait so they don't just flip the page.

8.1 Get creative with your environmental portraits.

8.2 Use your environment in creative ways for portraits.

Downplaying the background

The other approach to location is making it secondary to the subject. Portraits taken on white or black seamless backgrounds are a good example. These backgrounds focus all your attention on the subject, because there isn't anything else in the frame attracting your attention (**FIGURE 8.3**). Clean backgrounds like these work fine, and are especially helpful if you are dropping the portrait into another image for a composite shot.

Seamless backgrounds are great when you have to take a portrait in a location that doesn't help the image, such as an office or workplace. In this situation, you want to eliminate any sort of distracting background.

Establishing Rapport

"You have 15 minutes to get your shot."

This is the dreaded statement photographers hear more than they would like. You're hired to shoot a portrait, and the subject won't give you the time of day. Maybe they just don't have time and are in a hurry. To be fair, most adventure sports athletes I've photographed are very patient, and really nice. They often help me carry lights, offer me snacks, and show genuine interest in being there. No matter what portrait situation you encounter, the better rapport you have with your subject, the better the shoot will go.

Researching the subject

Good rapport begins with taking an interest in your subject. Maybe your subject is a famous rock climber with lots of difficult ascents to her credit. These are things you should know. But go beyond the obvious and research the subject. If the person is well-known, then you can find lots of information on the Internet. If there isn't much information available before the shoot, then you need to use your charming demeanor and engage the subject in conversation during the shoot. Find out more about their interests, family, and hobbies. Ask them details about the adventure sports activity they enjoy, such as, "What is your favorite route in the valley?" (**FIGURE 8.4**).

8.3 Solid backgrounds focus the viewer on the subject.

8.4 Research your subject before photographing them. Gauchos are "cowboys" of South America, and look good photographed in ranch scenes.

Multitasking on a photo shoot is a real art and takes time to master. Not only are you concentrating on talking with your subject so she feels at ease; you're also checking exposures, setting up lights, switching lenses, and wondering if that big cloud is going to dump rain on your shoot. The more comfortable you are with the technical aspects of the shoot, the easier it is to stay in touch with your subject. If your subjects feel you're not paying much attention to them, the shoot will go downhill. Establish rapport, and maintain it through the shoot. Bring an assistant or friend to help you set up lights or hold reflectors. That will let you concentrate on the subject.

Posing your subject

Start by being courteous and respectful to your subject. Your portrait subjects are letting you into their world, and trusting that you are genuine in your photographic approach (**FIGURE 8.5**). Show your subject respect, and be honest about your intentions. I always tell my subject what I have in mind and where an image might be used. If it's going to be a long shoot, bring food and drinks to keep everyone happy. Even the most shy or stoic person can be disarmed with a smile and a demonstration of genuine interest in who she is.

8.5 Work through many poses until you get the right look and feel for the shot.

Many people are uncomfortable being in front of a camera, and anything you can do to make them relax will help your shot. Posing them in familiar settings will put them at ease. I often find that subjects don't know what to do with their hands in a portrait, and they look awkward in the final shot. Give your subjects something to hold, such as a rope, paddle, or fly rod, and watch how they relax. Familiar objects will put them at ease (**FIGURE 8.6**).

One thing is very important to remember when you take a portrait: Be aware of subtle gestures, and follow your intuition. Every time I go into a portrait session, I have an idea in my mind for the shot. I research the subject, find an interesting background, and show up ready to shoot. I know what I want. But working with people is a dynamic situation, and you never know what will happen.

I start by posing my subject, and giving directions on what to do and how to look. As my subjects get more comfortable, they start doing things on their own, subtle gestures they do every day when they paddle or climb. These are moments you can't script, and often make the best portraits. Maybe you're shooting a kayaker who's holding her paddle as you direct her, and the moment we take a break, she starts holding her paddle another way. This is your shot!

I always ask my subjects for input on the pose and shot. They become more invested in the image, and generally have excellent suggestions for poses and locations.

8.6 Photograph subjects in settings that are familiar to them to make them comfortable.

THE IMPLIED PORTRAIT

Want to learn a creative portrait technique, something a little different? Try shooting *an implied portrait*. This technique involves shooting a portrait in which the subject can't physically be in the shot. How is this possible? That is where your creativity shines through. You could photograph your subject reflected in a mirror. Or maybe photograph objects that define the person, and have the subject's photograph in the frame. How about photographing her reflection in a pond? There are lots of ways to create the implied portrait, and this technique will get you thinking outside the box.

Effective Use of Light

As with any image, lighting is key to a successful portrait. If you're taking a portrait well off the beaten path, your options for artificial lighting may be limited. Remember that you don't need a truckload of lighting gear to create an evocative portrait. Effective use of whatever light is available is what counts.

Get the light right

When I approach a portrait, I think about the image concept. Who am I photographing? What makes him unique? What is the activity? Who is the end client for the image? Where am I going to be shooting the photograph? All these elements help determine what light is right.

At is most basic, lighting a portrait involves putting your subject in nice, available light and shooting away. This is more of a journalistic approach, quick and easy, and it won't intimidate your subject. At the other end of the spectrum is creating a portrait using overhead silks, reflectors, and multiple strobes, guaranteed to attract a crowd. You need to decide what light best supports your creative goals for the portrait, and what is possible given the subject and location (**FIGURE 8.7**).

Five ways to light a portrait

Below are five effective ways to light a portrait, from basic to advanced. Use these techniques as starting points for your own portrait lighting style. Decide what best works for your situation, and let your portrait evolve as the situation changes.

Available light

It doesn't get any easier than using available light in a portrait (**FIGURE 8.8**). Let Mother Nature do the lighting, and you can focus on posing the subject and directing the shot. Overcast light on a cloudy day is the easiest light to use. Since there are no shadows or direct sun, you can position your model anywhere and not worry about squinting or the angle of light. Look for good

locations that can add to the shot, and avoid including a lot of gray, pasty sky in the image.

Direct sunlight will add highlights and shadows in your image, similar to using a single light. Position your subject so she is not staring directly into the sun. Try side or backlighting for different looks. Shoot early in the morning or late in the evening to take advantage of the warm, flattering sunlight.

Sometimes, trees overhead act as natural diffusers for bright sun. Try placing your subject in dappled light under a tree for a different look using available light. Or put the subject on the edge of a shadow. She will have sun shining on her, but have a dark background behind her, creating nice separation.

8.7 Using available light and reflectors is quick and easy.

8.8 Using available light for a quick portrait.

One reflector

The next technique is using a simple reflector to help direct and modify the sunlight. Using a reflector (as discussed in Chapter 4, "Lighting in the Field") is simple, and won't overwhelm you with technical aspects so you can stay focused on your model. Position your model with sun at her back or to the side, and reflect light back onto her shadowed side. Control the intensity of the reflector by moving backward, and don't overpower the subject with reflected light. One of the biggest mistakes photographers make when using reflectors is eliminating all the contrast in the portrait. Add some fill light, but do so subtly and keep some shadow for a more interesting look. A soft gold/white reflector that opens to around 30 inches is all you need for waist-up portraits (**FIGURE 8.9**).

One speedlight and reflector

Of the two lighting methods we've discussed so far, we've used the sun as our light source. Add one speedlight, and you'll have two sources of light and a wide variety of lighting options. One of my favorite lighting techniques is using a speedlight aimed at a reflector to bounce nice, soft light back on my subject. Often I set my exposure so the sun will render an accent light on the back of my subject. The bounced speedlight adds soft, diffused light to the subject's shadowed front side.

A popular way of lighting a portrait is using a diffused speedlight (or other source) aimed at the subject from a high, slightly off-center angle (**FIGURE 8.10**). I use a Lastolite Ezybox with my Nikon SB900 and hold it high and to the side for many portraits. My camera is set to aperture priority and my flash is set to TTL in Remote mode. I trigger the flash using my SU800 wireless transmitter. This lighting style illuminates the subject in a flattering, wraparound, diffused light. Everybody looks good in this

8.9 A small, soft, gold reflector adds fill light in this image.

8.10 A small softbox used at a slight angle to your subject works well for many portraits.

8.11 A large softbox evenly lights close-ups.

CLAMSHELL LIGHTING

Imagine if you were photographing a subject with a really interesting face. Maybe it's a weather-beaten, craggy old climber, and his face tells the story of many years spent in the mountains. For this situation, *clamshell lighting* is a good technique. Clamshell lighting involves triggering a light high and frontal to your subject, and reflecting light back up directly below the subject using a reflector or other light source. If you use a softbox for the high light and a reflector for the bottom light, the set will vaguely resemble a clamshell. Clamshell lighting creates specular portraits with bright catch lights. Shoot right between the overhead softbox and reflector for a tight shot, or move your light and reflector farther away for waist-up compositions.

type of light, and it's a safe way to go for many portraits. If the sun is rim-lighting your subject, then you'll have created a simple cross-lighting scenario using the sun and one speedlight.

You can also use a snooted speedlight to create an edgy shot. Using a snoot narrows the angle of light to a small narrow band. Use a LumiQuest or Rogue snoot to narrow your flash, and aim it from the side to skim across your subject's face. If you don't have a snoot in your camera bag, roll up a piece of paper and tape it on the end of your flash. You'll be ready to go.

One large strobe

Using a large strobe instead of a speedlight enables you to use a larger, softer light source like a 53-inch diameter octabank. This lighting gear isn't as portable as a speedlight and reflector, but offers more power and incredible soft light. I generally use my Elinchrom lighting gear for any portrait that is taken close to the car. I love the quality of the larger light and the increased power. If I'm shooting in the middle of the day, I can overpower the ambient light with my Ranger pack and darken the background. The pack recycles very quickly so I don't miss a shot. For an intimate, close-up portrait of my subject, I use a big, soft source high and to the side of my subject (**FIGURE 8.11**).

If I want a more edgy look, I use a *beauty dish* on the strobe head. A beauty dish is a large circular white or silver dish that reflects light from the strobe head. These dishes produce a specular, edgy quality of light—not as soft as an octabank, and not as harsh as a standard reflector (**FIGURE 8.12**).

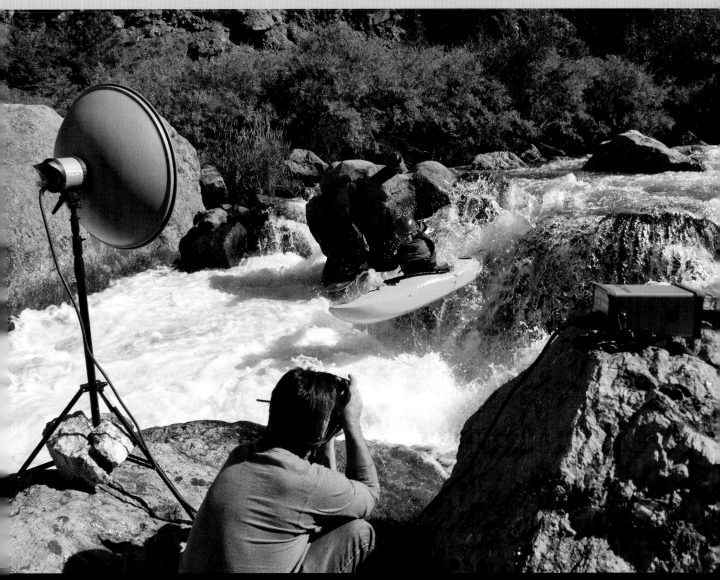

8.12 Using a beauty dish for a kayaking shot.

8.13 In this portrait, the background is underexposed to create separation and draw direct attention to the subject.

My normal portrait technique with a beauty dish or a softbox involves using the light center or slightly to the side my subject. I underexpose the ambient exposure by around 1 stop. I shoot in manual mode using large strobes. I like to change my ambient exposure via shutter speed rather than using exposure compensation on the camera, but either way works fine (**FIGURE 8.13**).

If I want to create a moody portrait, then I use a standard reflector on my flash head. This reflector produces deep shadows and bright highlights, and needs to be used carefully. Aim the light so you get shadows just where you want them on your subject. Be careful about producing shadows in the eyes of your subject. Use your reflector to reflect flash back into specific areas of your portrait.

Multiple strobes

If you have three lights or more, try some edgy lighting in your portrait. This technique uses a main light to illuminate the front of your subject, and two other lights each aimed at the side of your subject. The side lights will produce nice highlights on the side of your subject, and add contrast to the image. I normally start by setting my ambient exposure 1–2 stops underexposed. The background will still be obvious, but less important than the strobe-lit subject.

The trick to making this shot work is the power settings of your lights. Set the side lights to be 1 stop brighter than your main light so they create bright highlights. I use standard reflectors on the side lights, and a softbox as my main fill light. Experiment with your lighting ratios; it's OK to have

8.14 Using multiple flashes can give a portrait an edgy look.

blown-out highlights with some portrait lighting techniques (**FIGURE 8.14**).

Using three or more lights offers endless lighting possibilities. Try clamshell lighting using a softbox above and below your subject. Try placing one light with a standard reflector directly behind your subject to add a bright rim light, and use a softbox as the main front light source. Lighting is about experimenting; don't hold back.

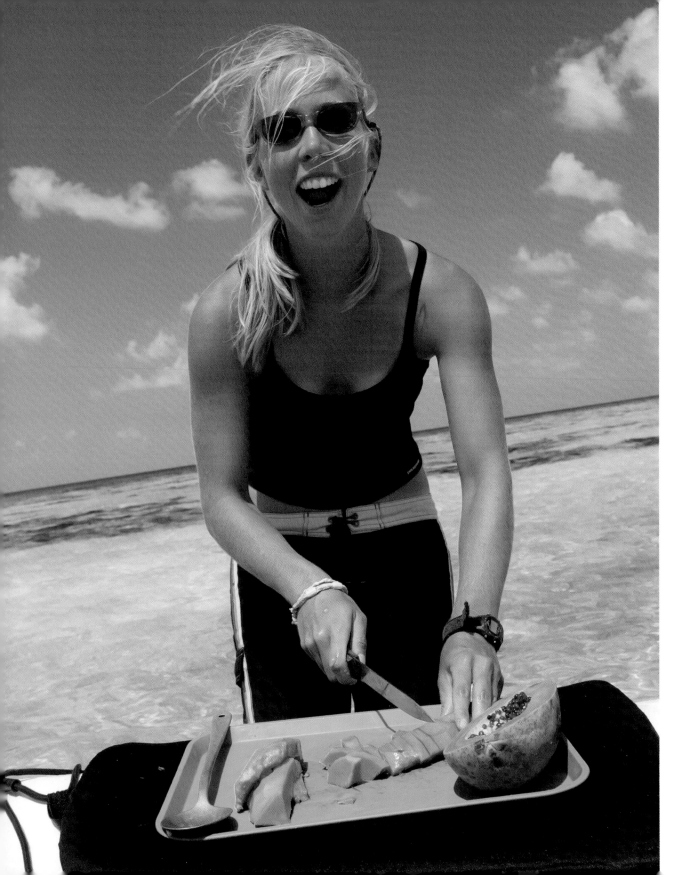

Impeccable Technique

Impeccable technique is just what it says. You need to be in control of your camera, not the other way around. In order to bring your creative vision to life, you need to know how to operate your camera. You may get some nice available-light portraits just shooting away, but flash portrait photography requires more technical know-how.

Depth of field

Choice of aperture and the corresponding depth of field is a major choice in any portrait. I choose my aperture based on two variables: subject sharpness and background sharpness. First, I need to use an aperture that will ensure my subject is sharp. If I'm using a 70–200mm lens and photographing my subject from a distance, then I can use a wide aperture opening like f/4 and get a sharp portrait. But if I use that same lens and aperture close to my subject and zoom in, then I need to focus on the subject's eyes. If I focus on her nose, the nose may be sharp, but the eyes will be soft. The other choice is to use an aperture with more depth of field like f/8 or f/11 to ensure both nose and eyes are sharp in a tight headshot using a telephoto lens.

The other important depth of field aspect is the background. When I create an environment portrait, I want the background to play a part in the image. I don't want my background so blurry no one can tell what it is. I choose an aperture that will either keep my background sharp, or make it slightly out of focus. The viewer will still be able to recognize the background, but it won't distract from the subject (**FIGURE 8.15**).

Creating separation between your subject and background is important. You don't want to have your subject merge with background elements; you want him to "pop off the canvas." Using an aperture that blurs the background but keeps the subject sharp creates separation in the image. Position your subject in the frame so that he's not in front of distracting elements, and eliminate *eye magnets* (distracting elements) in the shot. Adding flash to your subject and underexposing the background also helps create separation and a clean shot.

8.15 Choose the right aperture for the desired depth of field when shooting portraits.

CREATING SEPARATION

- Choose an aperture to keep your subject sharp and background slightly blurred.

- Position your subject on a clean part of the background without distracting elements.

- Add flash to your subject and underexpose your background.

- Position your subject in the sun against a shadowed background.

Shutter speed

Shutter speed is important for controlling the speed of background motion and ensuring a sharp photo. I normally prefer fast shutter speeds to freeze the action and eliminate camera shake during the shot. The exception to this is when I have moving subject matter in the background (**FIGURE 8.16**). I might decide to use a tripod and shoot at 1/4-second to render a background stream soft and silky.

Flash sync speed also affects what shutter speed I use. I like to stay at the maximum sync speed of my flash unless I need high-speed sync for the shot. Using your camera's flash sync speed doesn't require as much power as using high-speed sync. But if I need high-speed sync to darken the background or freeze the action with fill flash, I choose a fast shutter speed, such as 1/1000 and higher.

White balance

White balance controls the color temperature in your shot. Cameras have presets such as Auto, Sunny, Cloudy, Shade, Tungsten, Fluorescent, and Flash. Auto white balance works well for many situations, especially mixed lighting indoors. But if I'm shooting outside, I normally set my white balance based on the conditions. I use Sunny on sunny days and Cloudy on cloudy days. I use the Flash setting when I am using strobes. Matching the white balance to the environmental conditions results in a neutral color cast in the image. But neutral can be boring in portraits (**FIGURE 8.17**).

8.16 A fast shutter speed helps freeze the snow in this shot.

Sometimes I want my subjects to have a warm tone so I use the Cloudy white balance setting. This is similar to using a warming gel on your flash, but instead setting it on your camera. Other times I will add orange gels to my flash and set my white balance to Tungsten to produce moody blue backgrounds (Chapter 4). In the end, choose the white balance that supports your creative goal.

8.17 Choose your white balance based on the effect you want. A warm white balance was used in this sunset portrait.

Video

A lot of adventure sports photography is about story-telling. Maybe you're documenting an expedition to do a first descent of a remote river, or capturing a day at the crags. In your quest to create a visual story, you explore all options in capturing the event. And with today's modern cameras, shooting video is a great option.

Similar to digital still images, video quality has rapidly improved in recent years. Video was very basic on DSLRs when it was first introduced, a nice option but lacking a lot of important features. Now Hollywood directors are using DSLR video for segments in their movies.

Using an overhead crane to shoot a rock climbing video segment.

Many photographers are hesitant to shoot video because it encroaches on their still-image creation. I look at video as another form of media for accomplishing my creative goals in photography. I'll never lose my drive to create still images. Video just gives me another platform for demonstrating my skills, and incorporating moving images for a stunning visual journey. Since almost every new DSLR camera has video capability, why not give it a try and see what happens? You might just get hooked.

Shooting Video vs. Stills

Capturing video involves moving shots rather than a single still image. This is good, but also challenging for the photographer. On the one hand, you now have the opportunity to capture every moment of a scene. When the skier cruises past, you can capture every ounce of flying powder as he blasts through the scene. If you're recording sound, then you can add dialogue and background effects for a rich multimedia experience. Just think of the possibilities!

But capturing the scene completely also means you have to get it right for *the whole scene*. If you clip the skier's head at the end of the shot, then you have to reshoot. If your audio doesn't record properly, then you have try again. You can correct some mistakes in editing, but unlike stills that hinge on a single frame, great video involves thousands of frames (24, 30, or 60 per second!) *and* audio. You just have to be prepared and well organized for your shoot.

Creating a storyboard

A storyboard is a blueprint for your video, and can be very helpful in organizing your shoot. A storyboard will show diagrams of scenes, and detail the video and audio occurring in them. Before I shoot any multimedia piece, I sit down and look at the big picture. First, what is the video about, and what is the ultimate end goal for the shoot? Generally, I'm creating a story about the topic being covered, not shooting a few standalone clips. Don't assume you can shoot a short video for your client by just hitting the live view button on

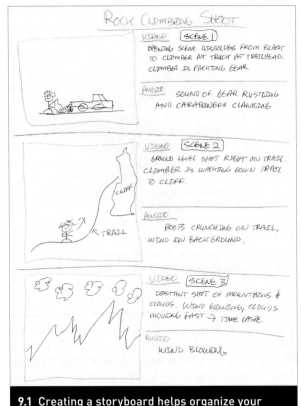

9.1 Creating a storyboard helps organize your video and foster creative ideas. As this diagram shows, you don't have to be a master sketch artist to sketch out rough ideas!

- Scene 2 will be a ground-level shot of the climber hiking down the trail, with audio of his boots crunching on the trail.

- Scene 3 will be a distant shot of the mountains and clouds racing past, with audio of the wind blowing.

- Scene 4 will cut back to the climber lacing up his shoes at the bottom of the crag, with audio from the climber describing why he likes to climb.

- Scene 5 will be a tight shot of his partner clipping into the belay device, with the audio capturing the sound of snapping carabiners.

- Scene 6 will be the climber chalking up and doing the first moves of the climb, with wind again providing audio in the background.

- Scene 7 will be a shot from above, zoomed in on the same section of rock, but showing a different angle, with the same audio as Scene 6.

- Scene 8 will be the climber putting a cam into a crack and clipping his rope to it, with the audio capturing the snapping of the carabiner.

After numerous clips and angles of the climb with audio narration in the background, you'll find yourself on your last few scenes. Scene 25 is the climber topping out on the route. The final scene shows the climbers coiling rope silhouetted against the setting sun fading to black, with audio of the wind dying away.

The outline for this simple video shows how complex a shoot can become. A storyboard will focus your ideas and improve your efficiency when shooting. It also forces you to think about specific angles and techniques you'll need to get the shot. Some climbing clips are going to be shot from above. That

your camera and recording away. If you take a random approach to shooting, that is how your video will look in the end—a random, incoherent grouping of clips.

Once I have my story defined, then I start writing down the various scenes I need to shoot to create the video (**FIGURE 9.1**). A typical storyboard for a day of rock climbing might go like this:

- Scene 1 will start black with the sound of clanking climbing gear and slowly dissolve into a scene of the climber packing gear at his car.

means you need to attach a fixed line to ascend to get above the climbers. This, in turn, means more time to rig the shot. You might also need a crane system to create a dynamic shot moving away from the face. Rigging a crane takes time as well; just getting this one clip might take hours.

All of a sudden, your simple one-day rock-climbing shoot might take two days to capture all the clips needed for the video. You may need a variety of lenses to get the right angles, and cranes and Steadicams to capture fresh perspectives. Always write a storyboard for your shoot; it will crystallize your creative ideas and identify the technical challenges of the shoot.

Video resolution and quality

Similar to digital still shooting, DSLR video involves numerous file and recording formats. Today's DSLRs offer a growing selection of video quality settings for recording your clips. These options include resolution, frame rate, and quality settings.

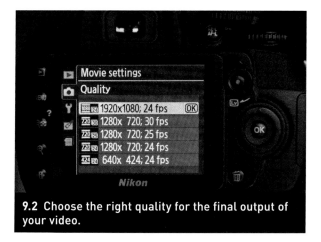

9.2 Choose the right quality for the final output of your video.

Resolution refers to the detail recorded during video capture. Standard-definition (SD) video has a resolution of 720 by 480 pixels (depending on video format), offering small file size but limited quality. Today, almost every DSLR offers high-definition (HD) video resolution for better quality. Two resolutions, 1280 by 720 (720p) pixels and 1920 by 1080 (1080p) pixels are common choices in video-capable still-image cameras. The larger file size of full HD 1080p video produces incredible quality, which is important if you're capturing video for viewing on a large HD screen cable of 1080 resolution. Shooting 720p HD also produces excellent video, and is all you need if you're going to show your video on the Internet (**FIGURE 9.2**).

Frame rate refers to the frames per second (fps) of capture. Typical frame rates choices on DSLRs are 24, 30, and 60 fps. Many photographers choose 24 fps when they want to simulate the look of film. This is the frame rate used for film movies, and thus offers the "cinematic feel" that many people like. On the other hand, 30 fps is the classic video frame rate and produces excellent HD video. Faster frame rates also do a better job of capturing quick panning shots and moving subjects. Slower frame rates can produce choppy video on a quick panning shot.

The quality setting on your camera refers to the compression rate of data the camera uses (specified as megabits per second, or Mbps). DSLR camera compression rates vary widely; one camera may use 12 Mbps, while another camera uses 48 Mbps. The higher the number, the better the quality. Choose the highest quality setting your camera offers. The files will be bigger, but you will have better video as a result.

Creating Dynamic Video

What's the big deal about shooting video with your DSLR? You can use your existing lenses for a variety of shots, and DSLR video offers a few advantages over standard video cameras. One major advantage is that a full-frame DSLR sensor is bigger than your normal video camera sensor. This allows more selective focus with blurry backgrounds for a moody shot, and low-light performance that puts even the best pro video cameras to shame.

Add to this the ability to use lenses ranging from fisheyes to 600mm telephotos, and you have an arsenal of tools to create dynamic video.

Keep it simple

The biggest mistake photographers make when starting to shoot video is trying to do too much. I speak from experience. When I got my first video-capable DSLR, I went wild working on my first video. I tried lots of moving shots, recorded multiple audio tracks, and added special effects in editing. The end result was a disaster! I needed to learn video technique slowly before I could expect to produce professional-looking movies.

Start with very short videos, maybe a few minutes in length, and keep things simple and straightforward. Create a storyboard with all the shots organized, as described earlier, and decide what extra gear, if any, your shoot will require. Draw on your still-image

- Create a storyboard to focus your ideas and determine camera angles and equipment needed.

- Use a solid video tripod to stabilize shots.

- Choose video quality settings based on your final output.

- Shoot a variety of interesting angles for more options in editing.

- Shoot both short and long clips to use in setting the pace of the final edited video.

- Shoot two or more angles of the same scene for dynamic coverage.

experience to know which lenses you'll use for specific shots. Begin with simple audio, or plan on recording no live or ambient audio at all during recording. Work on creating a video that will run with a music track you will add later in editing.

The only two tools you should need for your first video are a camera and tripod. Avoid attempting moving shots until you have mastered simple, static shots. Great video can be produced with clean, tripod-mounted shots. Do experiment with different lenses and depths of field; this is the joy of using your existing DSLR gear in shooting video. Use good available light to record your clips. As your video skills improve, slowly build more advanced technique into your production.

Use a variety of shots

Have you ever watched a video that consisted of nothing more than some person just standing there incessantly talking in monotone for what seems like hours? Your eyelids get heavy, you start daydreaming about some nice tropical beach, and the next thing you know, you're snoring! This is your worst nightmare for someone watching a video you produced! Mix up your coverage and keep things interesting (**FIGURE 9.3**).

Start by mixing up the shots in your video. The principles are very similar to covering a story by shooting stills. You might start with a *wide shot*, a scene-setter where the action will take place. Then you might take a mid-shot showing the subject. The next shot might be an *extreme close-up*, a close-up of a part of the subject such as her face or hands. Then you shoot a *cutaway*, a scene that doesn't show the subject but helps build the story. From here you go back to a *medium close-up* of subject. You get the idea. Mixing up shots keeps the pace of the video moving along, and keeps the viewer interested.

In addition to different angles, use short-duration clips to keep things rolling. Some clips may be only a few seconds in length, offering a very quick glimpse of a scene. Other clips might be 20 seconds long, as your subject completes a ski run or whitewater section.

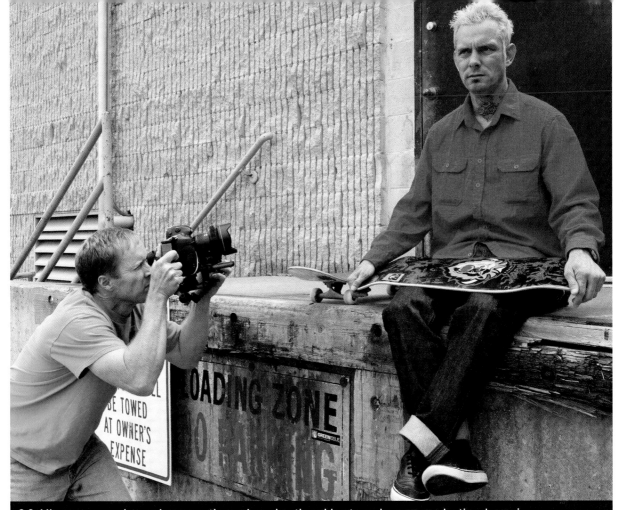

9.3 Mix up your angles and perspectives when shooting video to make your production dynamic.

Another technique is to shoot the same scene with two cameras at different angles. This allows you to mix up angles and clips while the subject is doing the same activity. If you don't have two video-capable DSLR cameras, see if your subject can do the same activity twice. When I shoot kayaking video, I like to capture one angle from the shore and the other angle from a head-cam. I will have the paddler do the run twice, once with the headcam capturing footage, the other time with the shore camera capturing video. This way I have two tracks I can mix together in editing showing the kayaker's perspective and the view from shore. I could just shoot this scene one time with the kayaker using the headcam, but it looks better if the paddler doesn't have a camera attached to his helmet as he paddles through the rapids.

Stabilize your camera

Despite the many popular clips we see featuring jerky camera movement, ranging from reality TV to some indie films to viral YouTube videos, stabilizing your camera will improve the quality of your video and avoid making the viewer nauseous. This doesn't mean you can't produce moving-camera shots; it simply means that your moving shots will be smooth and steady, the sign of a quality video production. You have many options for gear that will help stabilize your shot.

Video tripod head

The simplest way to stabilize your shot is using a tripod. Tripods are inexpensive, and one of the best investments for both still and video shooting. But your choice of tripod heads will be different for shooting stills and video. Video requires a head that is rock-solid when tightened, but offers smooth, fluid movements when you pan or tilt during a shot.

I use a Manfrotto MPRO 535 tripod with 504HD video head (**FIGURE 9.4**). The tripod has carbon-fiber legs, so it's light, yet stable for video shoots. The head is critical for producing clean video clips. I can slowly pan to the right or left with smooth, fluid movement due to the friction system used in the tripod head. Invest in a high-quality video tripod head; you won't be disappointed, and neither will your clients and viewers.

DSLR camera support system

What happens when you need to move with the camera during a shot? Obviously, using a tripod is out of the question. One quick and simple method for stabilizing your DSLR during a moving shot is holding the camera away from your body with the camera strap tight around your neck. This gives you a tripod effect and helps steady the camera. But this approach makes it hard to see the LCD for composition and focusing, and adds only a little stability when shooting.

A better choice for moving shots is a dedicated DSLR video camera rig (**FIGURE 9.5**). With the popularity of DSLR filmmaking, many companies have started to produce handheld and shoulder-mounted rigs to allow steady camera motion and functionality for moving shots.

9.4 A strong tripod and smooth head are critical for video production.

9.5 Using a Redrock Micro Stubling to stabilize a shot.

I use a Redrock Micro Stubling for many of my moving shots. This rig offers some significant advantages over hand-holding your camera. First, it's more stable. I use the handlebar grips, which give me great control and stability for the shot. Second, this rig has a follow-focus system that allows smooth, accurate focus during a shot. Finally, the Stubling allows easy viewing of my LCD monitor when I'm shooting, which is critical for focus and composition.

Steadicams and other stabilizers

If you really want to shoot a lot of moving shots, you might consider using a Steadicam or other stabilizer. A stabilizer rig will help minimize movement between the DSLR and the camera operator, even while they're moving. If you've ever watched a video of a person hiking up a trail in which the video steadily follows the subject, chances are the shooter used a Steadicam or comparable stabilizer to get the shot (**FIGURE 9.6**).

Since DSLRs are lightweight, a handheld Steadicam or other stabilizer works fine. I use a Blackbird stabilizer for motion-intensive moving shots. If I am going to be following a climber up the trail to the crag, the Blackbird works great to steady my camera as I record video hiking up the trail. Stabilizers take time to master, and need proper balancing to work correctly. But after a few shoots your stabilizer technique should be good enough to create smooth moving shots. Just be careful to watch where you are going when you are shooting video.

9.6 A Blackbird stabilizer produces smooth moving video.

Focusing the shot

Focusing with video works a little differently from focusing still shots. Since the camera is recording a continuous stream of data, the mirror in the camera must be flipped up during recording. In order for you to compose and focus the shot, you'll use your camera's LCD monitor for this task. Live-view mode turns on your LCD for continuous viewing for use during video recording.

Focusing can be challenging during video recording on your camera. If possible, I like to prefocus and figure out the composition before recording. I may use a wide-angle lens and small aperture opening to increase my depth of field in the shot. This reduces focusing problems, and keeps things simple. But you will want to focus during many of your clips. Some DSLR cameras have autofocus during video capture, many don't. This means you will be manually focusing during the shot.

The challenge of focusing using your LCD is that it is hard to see, and the resolution may not be high enough to determine accurate focus. One handy item I use is a focusing loupe, which eliminates glare and allows close-up viewing of the LCD monitor (**FIGURE 9.7**). I use an inexpensive loupe from Hoodman. This loupe has elastic straps that secure it over the LCD screen. The loupe is black, so even when I'm shooting on a bright, sunny day in the snow I get a clear view of my LCD screen.

The next step up in helping you focus and compose your shot is a monitor. A small 7-inch monitor can be very helpful in composing your shot. These monitors can be positioned right on the hot shoe of your camera, and tilted to right viewing angle. Monitors can also be attached to a DSLR video rig like the Redrock Micro Stubling or a Steadicam.

I use a M-LCD7-HDMI monitor by Marshall. This 7-inch monitor makes it really easy to compose and focus my shot. I can work with my camera at many different angles and still see the monitor. The monitor plugs into an HDMI port on my camera, and mounts on the hot shoe (**FIGURE 9.8**). One great feature is it uses the same batteries as my D300s.

9.7 A loupe will help in viewing your LCD screen for sharp focus.

9.8 Monitors offer large views of the scene for focusing and composition. They can be tilted for better viewing with low or high shots.

Recording Audio

Recording the picture part of your video is only half of the equation. Audio is just as important as the picture in a video piece. Audio helps set the mood and pace of the video, and provides important information in many videos. Imagine watching an interview without audio. Unless you're a lip reader, you're not going to get much out of it. Or consider this scenario: A kayaker approaches a big waterfall. You might not know this, but if the music starts building in tempo and you hear roaring water in the distance, you start sweating in anticipation of the big drop. This makes the shot much more impactful than it would be without the approaching roar of the waterfall.

Your options for recording audio range from using your camera's built-in microphone to adding high-quality external mics. Never discount the importance of audio; solid audio often separates the pros from the amateurs when it comes to video.

In-camera audio

The easiest way to record audio with your video is using your camera microphone. But while video quality has drastically improved with new cameras, audio quality has largely stayed the same. A big issue is that the in-camera mic often picks up unwanted noises. If your camera is focusing, or your lens image

stabilization is running, the mic may record this humming sound. Mic placement on the camera also affects performance. Some mics are positioned on the front of the camera, others on the top panel. While these mics can do well recording a conversation in a room, they pick up background noise as well. To solve these problems, it's best to use an external microphone.

External microphones

External microphones eliminate the problems in-camera microphones create. They don't pick up camera-handling or internal-camera noises. They can be directed to the source of the audio, or placed right beside the audio source. And external microphones have better sound quality than your average camera mic.

Shotgun mics

Since most adventure sports video recording will take place outside, a big challenge is recording just what you want your audience to hear and not the many peripheral sounds also occurring in the scene. To accomplish this task, a directional microphone is the best choice, and a shotgun works great (**FIGURE 9.9**). These microphones are designed to record audio where you point them, with minimal sounds recorded from the side. This works well for recording of a distant person speaking or a specific sound.

I use an inexpensive shotgun microphone by RØDE. This microphone attaches to the camera's hot shoe and plugs into the external microphone jack on the camera. The microphone has built-in shock

9.9 Using a shotgun microphone will minimize ambient noise and record audio coming from where you aim it.

absorbers to minimize camera and handling noise, and the sound quality is excellent. The microphone runs on a separate 9V battery. Just adding this microphone to your DSLR video setup will greatly improve the quality of your piece.

Lavalier mics

Another inexpensive way to dramatically improve your audio is to use a lavalier, or lapel, microphone. These small microphones attach to your subject's shirt at about chest level, putting him right at the audio source, which greatly improves sound quality. Lavalier microphones can be both cable and wireless. Wireless lavs can be very expensive, but they're convenient since you don't have to worry about the cord. But for $50 you can get a cable lavalier with excellent sound quality. I use an Audio-Technica ATR3350 lavalier microphone and get great results (**FIGURE 9.10**). I simply plug this microphone into the external microphone jack on my D300s and I'm ready to go.

9.10 A small lavalier microphone attaches to clothes for excellent sound quality.

Portable audio recorder

So far, we've looked at ways to improve the audio quality by using an external microphone, but still recording through the camera to the compact flash card. To take your audio quality to the next level, you'll need to use a portable audio recorder. These recorders offer much more control and a wider range of options in recording sound. A big benefit of a portable audio recorder is that it allows you to use sound bars to accurately adjust sound levels for the scene you're recording. You can also record in different formats such as MP3 or WAV format, and some models allow you to set different microphone patterns for varying recording scenarios.

I use a Zoom H2 portable recorder for most of my sound (**FIGURE 9.11**). This handy little device has great sound quality, records to an SD card, and has an LCD window to aid in adjusting sound levels. Better still, I can hook up a shotgun or lavalier

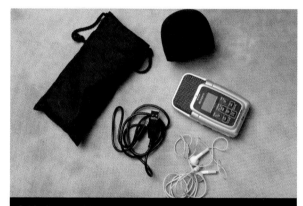

9.11 A portable recorder like the Zoom H2 offers more control and quality in recording audio.

microphone to further improve my sound quality. The audio track is then downloaded into your video-editing software and synced with your video.

When possible, use headphones when you're recording audio. Headphones allow you to accurately hear what is being recorded, especially useful in scenes with lots of ambient noise.

Video Lighting

Cinematography, like still photography, requires good lighting to make a quality movie. The difference in lighting video and stills is that video requires a continuous light source. Popping strobes light only one frame, but video records a continuous stream of frames. As with still photography, you have two choices: natural available light and artificial light that you can generate with continuous lighting for your video (**FIGURE 9.12**).

Natural available light

In Chapter 4, "Lighting in the Field," you learned about the characteristics of lights, and methods of controlling and altering natural available light. Here's the good news. Everything (well, almost everything) stays the same with using daylight to shoot video. The sun is your continuous light source; you don't have to worry about it turning off during the day (OK, maybe with an eclipse). You just need to think about how you might want to diffuse or reflect the light to your taste in the video.

9.12 Video requires continuous light sources from small LED light panels to larger fresnel lights.

A very handy light modifier for video is an overhead silk (**FIGURE 9.13**). Overhead silks diffuse the sun and create beautiful, softbox-like lighting on your subject. Add a few white reflectors to fill in any deep shadows, and you'll be ready to interview your subject in your outdoor studio.

One thing to watch for when using reflectors and shooting video is flicker. Many reflectors are not rigid, and the slightest breeze makes them bend and twist in the wind. This will affect the intensity of the reflected light on your subject and cause flickering. Use rigid reflectors when shooting video to avoid flickering light on your subject.

9.13 Using an overhead silk to soften sunlight works well for video lighting.

Artificial light

Artificial light for video has to be a continuous source. If you're trying to overpower the sun during a midday shoot, you're going to need a panel truck loaded with massive HMI lights and a bank account to match. Some Hollywood productions are doing this and using a DSLR to shoot some of the movie. But most of us are shooting small productions and need only a little extra light to help the shot. For that task, you can use simple hot shoe-mounted LED video light panels.

These light panels use numerous LED lights for illumination. The small-sized panels can be attached directly to your hot shoe, or attached to a light stand using a Justin Clamp. For the color temperature of the lights, you can choose tungsten or daylight. Some panels have the ability to change the color temperature on the unit. Larger 12-inch square panels have more power and can be tethered together to produce more light. These are mounted on light stands (**FIGURE 9.14**).

9.14 Small LED lights work well for lighting small video scenes.

I use a Litepanels MicroPro for artificial lighting on some of my video shoots. This light is about 4" × 5", runs on AA batteries, and is remarkably strong for its size. If I'm working in dim lighting conditions, it works well to add light to an interview subject. I can use two of these lights mounted on stands to create a simple cross-lighting setup for an interview. I can also modify the light quality by shooting through a small diffusion silk. LED lights stay cool, so you don't have to worry about making your model sweat.

If you need to light larger scenes, then you'll need larger light sources, and enough power to light them. There is a wide variety of makes and models of continuous light sources to match your needs. A few considerations with these lights include whether they can operate with batteries in addition to AC power, as well as what kinds of light modifiers are available to use with them. As with strobes, softboxes and grids can control your video lighting. Most large lights need AC power or large generators to power them.

Special Video Techniques

Now you have the core fundamentals you need to shoot good video in the field. Start by organizing your shoot with a storyboard. Choose the right video quality for your end use. Get a reliable tripod or stabilizing system for smooth shots. Attach a loupe or monitor to help with focus. Use a simple external microphone to improve your audio quality. Things are looking good.

Where do you go now? For starters, just keep shooting with the gear mentioned above. You have the right equipment, so from this point, your time is best spent mastering technique and shooting creative clips. Really focus on what new perspectives you can bring to your video to show the world a scene they haven't already seen. As with still photography, going through the creative process will refine your technique and creative vision.

But there are a few more techniques and tools that can give your video a creative, professional look. Experiment with these as you develop your video skills.

Tilt-shift lenses

One reason for the popularity of DSLR video among photographers is that it allows you to use your existing lenses to shoot video. And with large-sensor cameras, we can create blurry backgrounds using wide-open apertures like f/2.8. But there is a way to even further blur the background in unique ways and really add some mystery to a shot. Try using a tilt-shift lens.

Tilt-shift lenses can *tilt* or *shift* their lens plane, which allows you to exaggerate blur (or increase sharpness) in a shot. The area of sharpness can be off-center, giving you more creative control in the shot. Using this technique adds a lot of mood and mystery to a shot (**FIGURE 9.15**).

Another effect that changing the focus plane in the image creates is miniaturizing the scene. If you shoot a busy street scene from a high building, the cars, people, and road take on a miniaturized look. This can also be an interesting effect to add to a video.

Sliders

Moving video clips are just plain cool. The added motion in the shot makes it more interesting, and keeps the viewer engaged. But the challenge with moving shots is creating smooth, fluid movement, rather than shaky clips that look like you were falling down a hillside when you were recording the video.

Enter the slider, or portable dolly. These linear tracking systems use rails that allow you to move your camera slowly and smoothly for a moving shot. You don't need 10 feet of track to create an interesting shot. Slowly moving your camera a few feet during a clip will add a great effect (**FIGURE 9.16**).

I use a 3-foot rail system by Glidetrack. I mount my camera on a tripod head attached to the slider on the rail. The slider glides smoothly along the rail as fast as I push it. The rail can be placed on the ground or attached to a tripod. Make sure the rail is level or your movements will look tilted.

Overhead cranes

In most cases, video movements are limited to horizontal, moving shots, with only as much vertical movement as the shooter's height will permit. But how much interest could you add to your video by creating an elevated shot with the camera slowly rising, giving the viewer a new perspective of the scene? To create this shot you will need a crane.

9.16 A rails system like the Glidetrack allows you to add motion to your shot.

SKATEBOARD DOLLY

What happens if you want to do a moving shot that is longer than your slider can go? Movie dolly systems can be very expensive, but there is a $50 version at your local sporting goods store that's also known as a skateboard. A skateboard provides a rolling platform you can shoot video from by sitting or crouching on the board and having someone push you during the shot. Granted, this isn't nearly as controlled or stable as a professional dolly. But a skateboard can produce some great moving shots on any flat, hard surface.

9.15 Using a tilt-shift lens can create scenes with extreme out-of-focus elements.

9.17 A crane system allows you to shoot video above your subject.

Cranes work by attaching your camera to one end of the crane and adding weight to the other end to balance the setup. The crane is attached to a solid, smooth video tripod head. Cranes use a cable system that allows you to adjust the camera angle while the crane is in motion. Similar to a Steadicam, cranes take practice to get a smooth shot (**FIGURE 9.17**).

I use a CobraCrane Fotocrane Extreme. This crane can lift my camera 11 feet off the ground for dramatic shots. It weighs 7.5 lbs., which means it's light enough to haul on shoots in the backcountry. It takes only one person to operate. I use a wide-angle lens and small aperture opening on my camera to shoot from the crane since it doesn't focus while capturing video. Basically, everything from about 2 feet to infinity will be in focus with the aperture set to f/16.

Putting It All Together

This chapter has focused on field technique for capturing video. The other half of the equation is editing the video into an award-winning production! Learning video editing takes time and a lot of practice.

There are numerous video-editing programs you can use. Entry-level programs like Apple iMovie and Windows MovieMaker automate a lot of the process—essentially, you just drop clips into the program. But you will quickly find you want more control and options, and this requires a pro-level video-editing package like Final Cut Pro, Adobe Premiere Pro, or Avid Media Composer (**FIGURE 9.17**). To use these programs efficiently, you need a fast computer with lots of memory.

A great way to learn video-editing technique is through online training like Kelby Training (www.kelbytraining.com). You can watch these tutorials over and over until you have mastered the technique. Similar to learning Photoshop, mastering

video editing will allow you to express your creative vision in your multimedia production.

In the end, video is something every photographer will want to explore. Even if you think you're not interested, new cameras are offering more video-capture options with each new model, so the opportunity is right in front of you and will require little additional investment. And video gives you a great platform to show your still images synced to music or narration. Try it—you just might like it.

9.17 The other half of producing a video is editing your footage. This image shows the Final Cut Express timeline.

10

On the Office

After spending endless glorious days in the field creating award-winning images, what happens with all those photos back in the office? Are you going to make prints, upload to a website, or send them to a client? Or maybe all three? No matter what the end use, creating a reliable image workflow is a critical part of digital photography. Your workflow should include image editing and optimization, database management, and backup. In other words, organizing your pictures so you can find any image in seconds, and optimizing the shot so it looks good (**FIGURE 10.1**)!

Hanging out in the "office" during a sea-kayaking shoot in Belize.

Setting Up Your Workflow

Our office consists of computers against one wall, and a row of file cabinets on the other wall. Our image library includes over 250,000 images, with more than 100,000 slides stored in the file cabinets. And what's the best part? Within a minute we can find any image we have ever taken, all because we started and stuck with a sensible workflow for the past 20 years.

A typical day in our office consists of a client calling us with a stock image request. We quickly locate the file, do any image prep that's needed, and send it off to the client within minutes of getting the request. From a business standpoint, being organized and responsive to clients' needs is a big

10.1 We use Adobe Lightroom to database our images.

10.2 Image search results in our online database.

advantage. You may not need to be this fast at finding your images but, with a little organization, you'll have all your images right at your fingertips (**FIGURE 10.2**).

Back in the days of slides, things were simpler, but more laborious. I spent countless hours putting sticky labels on slide mounts to caption and organize them (**FIGURE 10.3**). On some assignments I would shoot 25 rolls of film a day for a week or more. This translated to 6,300 slides I would have to edit. My light table wasn't big enough! Today, shooting with digital cameras makes things much easier and faster. And I don't have to pay for film developing.

10.3 No more days of putting sticky labels on slides.

What software to use?

The first part of the workflow process is downloading the images to your computer and browsing the photos. Which shots are you going to keep and which ones are you going throw out? To make this process manageable, you need to select the application you'll use to browse, organize, and edit your images.

Many database applications are also browsers. Selecting one of these means one less application to use in your workflow, and brings up an important aspect of our approach that makes it much more efficient: Simple is good. Often, the more complex your workflow becomes, the less efficient it is. We have a simple workflow *and* we can easily find images. If you start to dread downloading your photos because of the time and energy required, this will ruin your workflow. I look forward to editing my images, and can easily process 20 GB of images in a day. Read on!

The software we use as the cornerstone of our workflow is Adobe Lightroom 3. Adobe really did a great job designing this software with lots of input from photographers. We can do 75 percent of what we need to do with an image in Lightroom alone. We do the other 25 percent of our work in Photoshop on more advanced image-processing tasks. And we use one other secret weapon in editing our images: Photo Mechanic (**FIGURE 10.4**).

Photo Mechanic is an image browser, not a database program. Why add another piece of software to our workflow? Because Photo Mechanic is fast— really, really fast. I can open a 16-GB flash card in Photo Mechanic and see image previews instantly. No more frustrating time spent waiting for pre- views to appear. Lightroom also lets you browse images, but not as fast as Photo Mechanic. This speed advantage may not be a concern for many pho- tographers, but when you're processing 20 GB of photos a day, extra speed is a beautiful thing.

10.4 Photo Mechanic is a lightning-fast image browser.

Workflow is a very personal, situation-dependent process. Everyone's shooting habits are different, and the approach you take will affect how you choose to set up your workflow and what software you use. Just remember to create a workflow that is organized and efficient, and one that works for you.

Downloading and adding metadata

The first part of editing your images is downloading them to your computer. You have two basic choices: Download the images directly into Lightroom from the flash card, or download them to your desktop, and then import them into Lightroom. If you're using Lightroom as your browser/database, then downloading the images directly into the program is the way to go. You might download images to your desktop if you want to do an initial edit using a browser like Photo Mechanic before importing the images into your database (we follow this approach when working with big batches of images). But if you are working with Lightroom, turn on the program before you insert your flash card/reader into your computer. Once the computer has recognized your card, Lightroom's Import dialog appears (**FIGURE 10.5**).

There are a number of important choices to make here. In the right column, you'll see four sections: File Handling, File Renaming, Apply During Import, and Destination (**FIGURE 10.6**). Configuring these settings is key to organizing your images at import for Lightroom. If you get it right when downloading images from the flash card, you'll have very little to do later in the workflow.

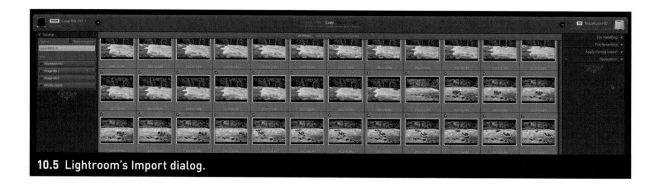

10.5 Lightroom's Import dialog.

The first step is to set File Handling properties. In the Render Previews box, you have four choices in the size and quality of previews you see during editing. I use Minimal. This setting uses the smallest embedded preview in the image, and is the fastest. Choosing a larger preview such as Standard gives you a larger preview, but takes more time to render. For me it's all about speed, so I go with Minimal.

Below the preview setting is a check box that allows you to download your images simultaneously to a second hard drive. I always have this check box selected, and choose a second hard drive for the images to go to so that they're downloaded *and* backed up at the same time to a second drive.

The next setting you need to address is File Renaming. You have a variety of choices available in the template box using file names, custom names, dates, and the like. This is a very important part of your database organization, because all of your individual images will have these names attached to them. I use Custom Name-Sequence. This setting allows you to use a name or acronym for the subject matter and an individual file number. For example, I use "raft" as my acronym for rafting images, and tag a sequential file number on the end. Each time I add new rafting images to my database, I start with the next number from that last rafting image in my database. I like this method because if I find files on disks or drives, it allows me to instantly recognize what the subject matter is. A meaningless series of numbers would make this impossible. With database search capabilities, this type of file naming isn't necessary, but it works seamlessly with our previous method of labeling slides (**FIGURE 10.7**). I leave the file extension as is in this box.

The Apply During Import setting gives us the most work to do. First is the Develop Settings box, in which you can choose a wide variety of processes to apply to your images. I leave this box alone since I do this type of image work later in my workflow. Below this box is the Metadata box, and this is where the real power of a database lies. Metadata consists of tagged information about your photograph. EXIF data is shooting data like shutter speed and aperture that's inputted by the camera. IPTC data is captioning and keywording data tagged to the shot by the photographer. A database search engine like Lightroom uses this data as criteria for searches. The more information you add here, the more accurate your image searches will be.

10.6 Set these variables at import.

10.7 My file-naming system uses a custom name-sequence style.

In the Metadata box, choose New, and a metadata preset window pops up (**FIGURE 10.8**). This window contains numerous fields in which you can add information about your shot. I always add a caption, copyright information, and keywords to every shot. There are numerous other areas where you can add information, but I normally don't use them. Remember, this is your chance to add appropriate keywords that you can use to search when looking for this image. Once you have this window filled in, you can save it as a preset for future use. My rafting metadata would be very similar except for the location. Saving a rafting metadata preset would make captioning these types of images much quicker the next time around.

The last category to address when downloading your images is choosing their Destination. This menu allows you to choose where the original image will live on your computer. Navigate through your computer and select the exact hard drive and folder location for your images. Let's look at the rafting images as an example. First, I would direct these pictures to my image hard drive (a drive reserved just for images on my computer). Next, I route the images to my Images folder on the same hard drive, and finally the photos go into the Rafting subfolder within this folder.

I have multiple hard drives installed on this main computer. This allows me to select one drive where my images will be stored. Remember how, in File Handling, we simultaneously downloaded to a second hard drive? This drive is an external hard drive that I keep out of the office for more security. If my main computer crashes, I have my images on another drive in a different location.

This may seem tedious to set up, but once you've started downloading images via Lightroom to your computer, it gets very easy. The best part is that you're getting all your captioning information done at this point in your workflow. You may decide later to further organize images into smaller collections, but the bottom line is this: If you've added the necessary metadata at import, your images are only a quick search away in Lightroom.

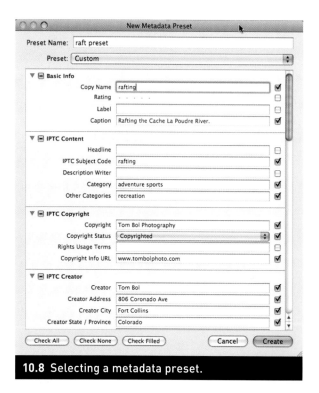

10.8 Selecting a metadata preset.

Editing Your Images

Now you've downloaded your images onto your computer. Nice going. This is where the fun really begins! Watching images pop up on the screen the first time is like watching the Superbowl. The excitement and anticipation is palpable. Did the shot come out like I thought? Was the light really that good? Were there any surprise images, good or bad? The beauty of digital photography is that you get quick results. No more sleepless nights spent wondering if your assignment shots came out!

Lightroom has five modules: Library, Develop, Slideshow, Print, and Web (**FIGURE 10.9**). Library is the editing module, and probably the one you will use the most. This window should already be open after you have downloaded your images.

10.9 Lightroom's five modules.

As an editing browser, Lightroom gives you numerous methods of selecting, rating, and deleting your images. What method you use will directly correlate to the amount of images shot and how much time you have to edit them. If you have only 100 images from a family vacation, you may use the Star rating system available for each image. Once you've rated the images with stars, you can search for star-rated images using the search fields (we'll look at that next).

As I mentioned earlier, because I shoot a lot of images, I keep my editing very simple. I either choose an image, or I delete it; no middle ground allowed. This may sound harsh, but it's the most efficient way for me to edit thousands of images at a time. In Lightroom, to choose an image to delete, I hit the shortcut key P, which flags the image. When I'm done with my edit, I select all the flagged images and delete them from Lightroom.

Lightroom offers choices when you delete photos (**FIGURE 10.10**). You can delete the image from Lightroom but still have it on your hard drive, or you can delete it from both Lightroom and the disk. I choose to delete the shots from both. If I don't like the shot or it's technically off, then I toss it into the trash, just as I would have done with a slide.

Is this method for you? Maybe. Does it have some drawbacks? Maybe. Is it fast and efficient? Yes. Perhaps your journalistic shot captures a person who later becomes famous. When you shot it, the image meant nothing, but later it has a lot of value. Or maybe digital processing will progress and allow us to fix images that today we would throw out. These are all possibilities that I can live with in my editing.

Another topic arises here as well. Where do you draw the line on keeping or chucking an image? Maybe the shot has sentimental value, and you'll keep it even though the exposure is off. Maybe the shot is just a little blurry, so you deem it good enough to keep.

10.10 Lightroom offers choices for deleting an image.

There is no right or wrong answer here; how you approach workflow and editing is your decision to make. If you're sending images to clients, then your standards are different than if you're shooting images for your personal scrapbook. My shooting ratio varies depending on what the subject is. If I'm shooting fast-moving sports, then I may only get 1 image out of 20 that I really like (**FIGURE 10.10**). If I'm shooting static landscapes, then my ratio will be better.

I also apply this to long time frames. Each year, I hope to get 5–10 spectacular shots that really define my work as a photographer. After a decade of

10.11 Fast-action photography results in only a few good shots among hundreds that are taken.

shooting, I might have 10–20 images that are published over and over again. These are my iconic shots, the ones I try to capture every time I pick up a camera.

Searching for your image

One of the strengths of Lightroom is its ability to search for an image. Users can search by almost any image characteristic: lens, camera, date, subject, what mood you were in...well, almost! Searching for an image in Lightroom is easy.

Start by opening the program and going to the Library module. Just click on this in the upper right or use the shortcut key G. Next, in the left column, make sure you've chosen All Photographs to search all your images. With the Library module open, you will see four categories at the top of the image previews: Text, Attribute, Metadata, and None. Let's start with Text (**FIGURE 10.12**).

10.12 Search options in Lightroom.

Choosing Text reveals two drop-down boxes and one box for entering key-words. The drop-down boxes offer many choices for narrowing your search. In the first drop-down menu, I normally choose Any Searchable Field and, in the second drop-down menu, I choose Contains All. These choices tell Lightroom to search the entire database for whatever word we enter in the last box. If I want to look for canoeing images, I just type *canoeing* into the last box. Presto, all my canoeing images will appear. I could narrow this search down by selecting more specific categories in the drop-down menus, but I can get search results fast by just typing in the subject. In a few seconds Lightroom will have found images in a database of over 100,000 images.

There is a way to further search the canoeing images I have just found. On the far right of the window is another drop-down window labeled No Filter (**FIGURE 10.13**). This menu allows you to further search these images using other criteria listed in this menu. For example, if you choose Camera Data, a new window appears showing all the EXIF data of the images found in this search. If you choose a specific camera or lens listed in the metadata, only the images shot with that camera or lens will appear. Using this method, I can narrow my search even further.

The next option is Attribute. Attribute searches information you add when browsing your images. Lightroom allows you to add flags, colors, and star ratings to images to help in editing. In the Attribute drop-down window you can choose to view only the flagged images you chose in your edit.

The Metadata search option is just plain cool. When you select Search Metadata, a new window appears, showing you the Date, Camera, Lens, and Label categories (**FIGURE 10.14**). You just choose what camera you would like to see images from, and wham, up come all the images shot with this camera. The same can be done for any metadata field shown in this window.

I write for a number of photography magazines, and they often do stories revolving around using one specific type of lens. Just the other day, a photo editor asked me to send him a selection of landscape images using a 70–200mm f/2.8. First, I entered *landscape* in the Text field to tell Lightroom to find all the images I had tagged as "landscape." Next, I selected the Filter drop-down window and chose Metadata. In the Metadata dialog, I chose the 70–200mm f/2.8 lens. In less than a minute I had found the images I was looking for from a huge database of images. Lightroom is amazing.

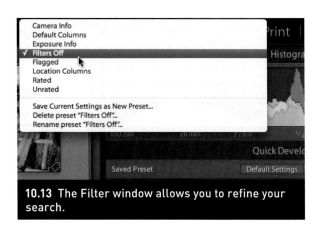

10.13 The Filter window allows you to refine your search.

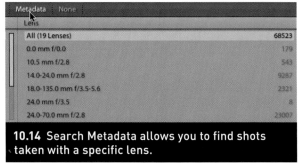

10.14 Search Metadata allows you to find shots taken with a specific lens.

Six Ways to Optimize Your Images

Now that you have downloaded, edited, and added metadata to your images, the next step is optimizing your shots so they look good. I define image optimization as doing baseline processing on every shot that is being used. I don't do all these steps with every shot I download; I optimize only the ones I am using. If a client calls for a specific shot that isn't optimized, I process the shot before it goes out the door. All my image optimization takes place in Lightroom in the Develop module (**FIGURE 10.15**). I switch into Photoshop to do more advanced processing like creating selections and using Layer Blend mode, but generally, I find that I can do everything I need to do in Lightroom.

10.15 Lightroom's Develop module.

10.16 Image optimization will bring your digital image to life.

So far we have worked in the Library module in Lightroom. Now we're going to move into the Develop module to optimize the shots. Click on the image you want to work on to select it, and choose the Develop module.

When I'm working in Lightroom's Develop module, there are six things I do to every shot that goes out the door: dust-spot, adjust exposure, set white balance, set white and black points, adjust curves, and sharpen. If you get good exposure with the right white balance in-camera, these adjustments will be minimal. But RAW digital images need a little touch-up to get them to the same level as a slide had when it was developed (**FIGURE 10.16**).

Dust spot

One of the most exciting things I do in the office is create 13" × 19" prints from an image. I practically vibrate with excitement watching the print come to life, as it emerges slowly from the printer. Halfway through the print I'm high-fiving my office help. Then, as the last inch of the image emerges from the printer, I see something in the blue sky. Could it just be some weird reflection in the office? No, it is a big, black UFO dust spot in the shot. My high point just turned into a low point.

Most cameras today have sensor cleaning, and I use mine religiously. I'm careful in the field when changing lenses, and I try to minimize any dust that might enter my camera. But no matter how careful I am, I get dust on my sensor. Don't let your concern over getting dust in your camera prevent you from switching lenses in the field. If you need a different lens for the shot, then switch it. Better to capture a dusty image than no image at all. You can remove dust later in Lightroom.

In the Develop module, the dust removal tools are located just below the histogram in the right column. The tool icon is a circle with an arrow coming out the right side. When you click on the tool, a window appears below it.

To begin, you have two removal actions, Clone and Heal. The Clone option copies exactly what is sampled by the tool, while the Heal option tends to blend and copy what is sampled. I use the Heal option in this example because the brush does a better job of seamlessly eliminating dust spots.

Below these options are Brush size and Opacity. Choose the brush size that works for your spots, and leave opacity at 100 percent to fully eliminate the spots. The tool works by simply putting the crosshairs cursor over the dust spot and clicking. The tool samples a nearby similar area and eliminates the dust spot. The best part is that Lightroom remembers your dust spotting. The next time you open this image in Lightroom, the dust spotting will be visible (**FIGURE 10.17**).

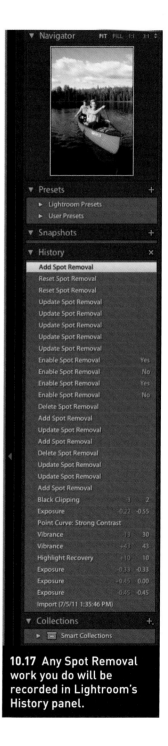

10.17 Any Spot Removal work you do will be recorded in Lightroom's History panel.

Adjust white balance

White balance is a quick fix, but an important one. You can set a specific white balance in your camera such as Cloudy or Daylight and be good to go. But when you open your images, you may decide you want to adjust this aspect. White balance can be very important to some projects such as catalog shoots where clothes have to be the right color.

But when you're shooting adventure sports, white balancing is more intuitive than scientific. The White Balance tool is located right below the Spot Removal tool. There are two sliders, one for temperature and the other for tint. Beside these sliders is a drop-down menu showing a variety of preset white balances (**FIGURE 10.18**).

How do I determine the *correct* white balance? By reviewing my image on my calibrated monitor and moving the temperature slider until it looks good. I may warm up my landscapes, change my star trails to incandescent, and add a little warmth to a portrait.

The bottom line is that today's cameras often get very close to the right white balance at capture, so I usually don't have much to do here. This is a subjective choice to a large degree. I try to keep things fairly accurate to the way I remember them in the field.

10.18 Use the White Balance slider and presets to adjust white balance.

Set white/black points

Below the White Balance sliders is another set of sliders. The two that I use most often are the Exposure and Blacks sliders. The Exposure slider helps me adjust just that—the exposure. In particular, I can drag this slider to the right and brighten up my image. But remember, as amazing as Lightroom is, and as effective as its corrective tools are, you should always try to get the right exposure in the field. You can adjust exposures only so far before the image degrades.

Once I've set the slider so the exposure looks right, I look at the histogram and see if there is a gap on the left side of the histogram. If the histogram doesn't reach the left side of the graph, I move the Blacks slider to the right and stretch the histogram to the left. This resets the black point in the image and, more importantly, it adds color and contrast to the shot. You know how some images just look flat and almost hazy? Adjusting the Blacks slider often is all that's needed to make the image pop.

Add vibrance

The Vibrance slider is the coolest tool of the bunch. It really should be renamed the smart saturation tool, because adjusting saturation intuitively is what it does. The Vibrance slider is right below the Clarity slider (**FIGURE 10.19**). Dragging the Vibrance slider to the right will increase saturation where the program thinks saturation is needed. This adjustment typically doesn't affect skin tones, and it often really punches up color in skies. I almost always add a little vibrance to my shots.

Adjust curves

Located below the Vibrance slider is the Tone Curve adjustment window (**FIGURE 10.20**). Adjusting curves will add contrast and saturation to your image. I always experiment with curves when processing my images. I may not like the effect, but it's worth looking at on each shot you plan to optimize.

To adjust curves, I start by choosing one of the preset curves in the drop-down window at the bottom right. I start with Medium Contrast and see how the image looks. This is often the best choice, but occasionally very flat images look better using the Strong Contrast option. To fine-tune this adjustment, I will adjust the sliders in this window to target areas that need more contrast.

Sharpen the image

I saved the best for last. Since I shoot in RAW format, my Nikon NEFs need sharpening to be their best. I don't have any sharpening turned on in the camera. As a rule of thumb, I try to do most of my processing in Lightroom, not in the camera. The one exception to this is long-exposure noise reduction (as mentioned in Chapter 6, "Photographing Mountain Sports").

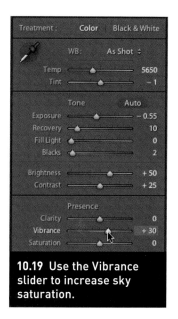

10.19 Use the Vibrance slider to increase sky saturation.

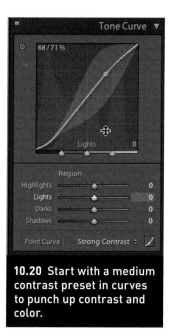

10.20 Start with a medium contrast preset in curves to punch up contrast and color.

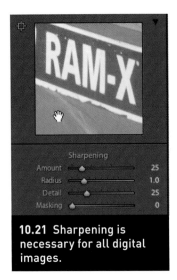

10.21 Sharpening is necessary for all digital images.

The sharpening sliders are located in the Detail window in the Develop module (**FIGURE 10.21**). There are four sliders: Amount, Radius, Detail, and Masking. The Amount slider will control the strength of the sharpening. What this really does is increase edge contrast, which adds the appearance of sharpening.

The Radius slider affects how far the contrast goes out from the selected pixels. The Detail slider affects the amount of details sharpened. A high number like 100 targets all pixels as detail and sharpens them all. A lower setting will identify fewer pixels as detail and sharpen less of the photo. The Masking slider allows you to select certain areas of the image to receive minimal sharpening. Imagine a portrait with lots of skin tones. You don't want to sharpen continuous areas of skin; this makes skin look grainy and textured. By increasing the Masking slider, these continuous-tone areas will receive less sharpening. Holding down the Alt/Opt key while adjusting the Masking slider shows you exactly what is being masked out.

To sharpen an image, begin by making sure you have the preview box open. To open this box, click on the triangle in the upper-right corner of the Detail window. The preview box shows you a 100-percent view of your image, allowing you to accurately gauge your sharpening efforts.

I start by increasing the Detail amount until I see noticeable sharpening occurring. The same applies for the radius amount. The goal is to sharpen the image, but not go overboard and add noise to your shot. Images vary on the amount of sharpening they require depending on the subject matter. A forested hillside will require different settings than a portrait. Experiment until your image looks good.

Backing Up Your Images

At this point, you should be feeling good. You've set up an efficient workflow, downloaded images, and optimized the shots. You're ready to print images, send them to friends via email, or upload them to a client's ftp site. But what would happen if, right at this moment, your computer crashed? If you followed the steps on downloading your images earlier in this chapter, you

should be covered, because you saved the images on another drive while downloading into Lightroom. The last part of your organizational workflow should include backing up your images to at least two different locations.

What are your options for backing up images besides storing them on your main computer? External hard drives, third-party server storage, and archival disks will all work. Today, hard drive space is very inexpensive. Buying 1-terabyte external drives provides lots of space for minimal cost. These drives can also be stored away from your home or office for more security. Another option is a RAID system that has multiple mirrored drives in a single unit. Redundant drives copy all incoming data for safekeeping on multiple disks. I use multiple hard drives in my office as a way of backing up images. One drive is on the computer and the backup external drive is stored in another location. I have never had a hard drive failure.

Another option is using an online third-party service such as PhotoShelter or Carbonite. These companies will allow you to store your images for a fee. The pricing is based on the amount of space you need. These servers have redundancy built into their backup systems, and many use a RAID system. All your images are stored offsite.

We have an online keyword-searchable database built into our website. This database has thousands of images clients can search for projects. Viewers can create lightboxes, send them to clients, or reference them later. I can create lightboxes on the road and send them to clients for image requests. Having

online access to my images is very convenient for submitting images to photo editors (**FIGURE 10.22**).

Another option is using archival DVDs. Delkin makes discs that are projected to have a shelf life of around 100 years. These discs work fine, but you will need a lot of DVDs if your files are large. And who knows how long computers will still be able to read DVDs!

ONLINE PHOTO DATABASES

Online photo storage is an excellent option for backing up your images. Carbonite, PhotoShelter, and Smugmug are just a few examples of online image backup. These services offer personal websites, online image-search capabilities, and redundant backup systems. Better still, you can access your photos while traveling on the road. Monthly fees vary depending on how much space you need. Many sites enable you to sell your images as stock photos. All you need to do is start uploading your images.

Another strategy for backing up data involves storing your images on two different hard drives, and archiving your best images from these files in a third location like an online backup service. This way, you won't need as much online space, and your best work will be secure in a third location. You must decide your comfort level with backup. I'm happy with images in two drives in different locations. So far, so good!

FIGURE 10.22 Online databases are a great way to access your files on the road.

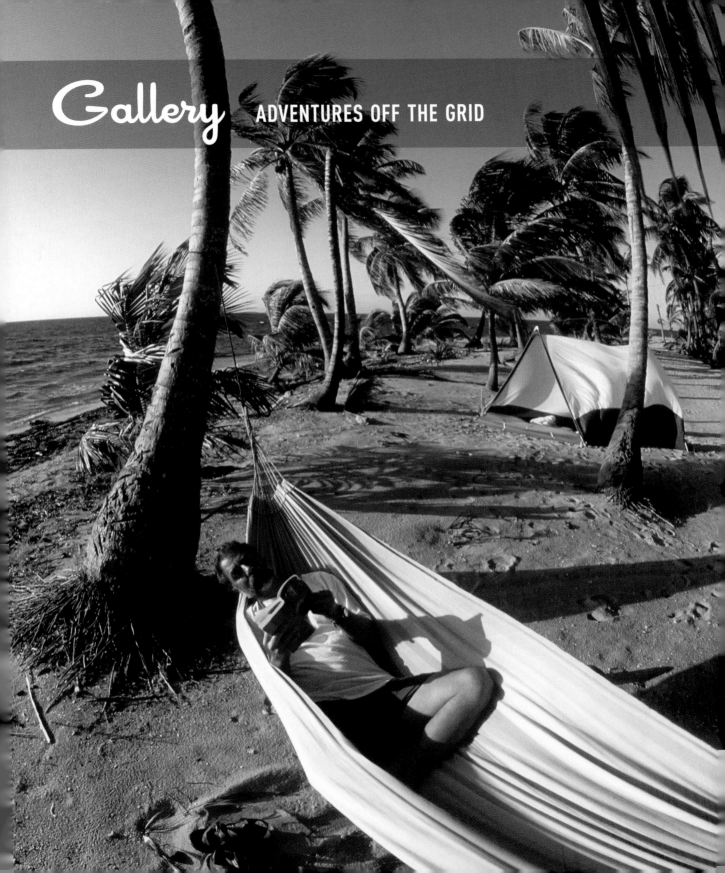

DOG
TEAM
XING

Index